"Will whet appetites of fans of both *Iron Chef* and *Murder, She Wrote*."

—*Booklist*

wine while enjoying the adventures of Benjamin Cooker in this terrific new series."

—*William Martin, New York Times bestselling author*

"An excellent mystery series in which you eat, drink and discuss wine as much as you do murders."

—*Bernard Frank, Le Nouvel Observateur*

"An enjoyable, quick read with the potential for developing into a really unique series."
—*Rachel Coterill Book Reviews*

"I finished it in one sitting! I learned so much about wine making…. But more than that is was a good little mystery—nothing wasted. The book would be perfect for a book club to have a 'wine' night."
—*Bless Your Hearts Mom*

"A fine vintage forged by the pens of two very different varietals. It is best consumed slightly chilled, and never alone. You will be intrigued by its mystery, and surprised by its finish, and it will stay with you for a very long time."
—*Peter May, prize-winning, international bestselling author*

"This is an excellent translation. You never have the feeling you are reading a translated text. The author obviously knows Bordeaux extremely well, and he knows quite a bit about oenology. The book should be a hit with lovers of Bordeaux wine."
—*Tom Fiorini, The Vine Route*

Nightmare in Burgundy

A Winemaker Detective Novel

Jean-Pierre Alaux
&
Noël Balen

Translated from French by Sally Pane

LE FRENCH BOOK

First published in France as
Cauchemar dans les Côtes-de-Nuit
by Jean-Pierre Alaux and Noël Balen
World copyright © Librairie Arthème Fayard, 2004

English translation copyright ©2014 Sally Pane

First published in English in 2014
by Le French Book, Inc., New York

www.lefrenchbook.com

Translation by Sally Pane
Copyediting by Amy Richards
Proofreading by Chris Gage
Cover designed by David Zampa

ISBNs:
Trade paperback: 978-1-939474-05-6
Hardback: 978-1-939474-28-5
E-book 978-1-939474-27-8

*"O happy Burgundy, which merits
being called the mother of men since
she furnishes from her mammaries
such a good milk."*
—Erasmus

1

His head was spinning. For three hours now, he had been sitting at the table between the wife of the ambassador to the Netherlands and a film star whose name he dared not ask for fear of offending her. He vaguely remembered having seen her in a period piece where she played the harpsichord in a château full of mirrors and china. He had to lean in a bit to exchange a few words with the guests across from him. Bunches of red and yellow tulips cluttered the tables. People smiled at each other between the stems.

The dinner was sumptuous, as elegant as it was generous. You could read the satisfaction on the faces of the guests. As the feast continued, attitudes relaxed, looks of collusion replaced polite nods, and witty remarks cut the air with great panache. After savoring a duck pâté accompanied by a Bourgogne Aligoté des Hautes Côtes, perch supreme served with a chilled and fragrant Meursault, and crown loin of veal sprinkled with green peppercorns, along with a 1979 Côte de

Beaune Villages, the guests thought the meal was finished. But this was underestimating the hospitality of the venerable knights of the Confrérie des Chevaliers du Tastevin. A cockerel and morel fricassee seasoned with Chambolle-Musigny added to the feast, and no one had trouble finishing it. Meanwhile, the Cadets of Bourgogne, decked out in black caps and wine-merchant aprons, had accompanied the arrival of each dish with a great many wine songs, comical tales, and jovial melodies. Beaming, with sparkling eyes and gleaming whiskers, they bellowed verse after verse at the top of their lungs.

Always drinkers, never drunk,
They go along their way
And thumb their nose at fools who grump.

Always drinkers, never drunk,
They happily proclaim
Their credo without shame.

Always drinkers, never drunk,
They go along their way!

The cheese course was announced. Platters arrived filled with creamy Epoisses washed in marc brandy and aged on rye straw, a soft farmhouse Soumaintrain cheese, mild Saint-Florentin that gave off the scent of raw milk, lightly salted and creamy Chaources, and supple La-Pierre-qui-Vire. Accompanying them were small rounds of goat's milk cheese, including an especially full-bodied tomme du Poiset. To top it off and honor this Chapter of the Tulips, the hosts had elegantly slipped in some soft Dutch cheese with amber and orange hues. Benjamin Cooker prepared a nice plate for himself, enhancing it with a 1972 Latricières-Chambertin that sensuously tickled his taste buds.

Here come the Cadets of Burgundy,
Sowers of life and of sun;
Lovers of water are mad.

Here come the Cadets of Burgundy,
A bottle in each hand!
Open the door to some fun
Here come the Cadets of Burgundy,
Sowers of life and of sun!

The chamberlain stepped to the podium. The association's slogan—Never whine! Always wine—was inscribed above it in gothic letters.

He tapped the microphone, waited for the brouhaha to subside, and greeted the assembly. He congratulated the chef for the excellent dinner and declared the meeting of the Chapter of Tulips open. Then, in a solemn voice, he briefly praised Benjamin Cooker, introducing him as the most recognized wine specialist in France and one of the most sought-after winemakers in the world. He spoke of the *Cooker Guide*, whose publication all vintners dreaded, and emphasized that the most recent edition had excellent evaluations of certain Vougeots. Finally, he invited the inductee to join him on the stage, next to the members of the association whose gold and red vestments shimmered in the spotlight.

There was a ripple of applause. Leaning on the edge of the table, Cooker rose slowly. He emptied his glass of water, discreetly loosened his bowtie, tugged down the jacket of his tuxedo, and made his way between the tables. He felt the weight of all the eyes turned toward him and slowed his pace a bit for fear of getting tangled in the train of an evening gown or tripping on a chair as he made his way to the dais. He was welcomed with a quotation recited with good-natured pomposity. The crudeness of its kitchen Latin made all the guests laugh.

> *Totus mundus trinquat cum illustro pinot*
> *Imbecili soli* drink only water!
> So, Brother Cellarer, fill our cup
> Because, as the saying goes: *in vino veritas*

Cooker was handed a chalice. He emptied it and proceeded to the dubbing, which fell somewhere between schoolboy farce and ritual solemnity. He swore fidelity to the wines of France and Burgundy and then bowed his head while the grand master of the order tapped his shoulder with a vine shoot.

By Noah, father of the vine
By Bacchus, god of wine
By Saint Vincent, patron of vintners
We dub you Knight of the Tastevin!

Cooker was then invited to take the microphone. He looked over the assembly, and a silence as thick as a wine coulis filled the room. One last clearing of the throat, and his voice resounded under the enormous girders of the wine warehouse.

"Grand Chamberlain of the Order of the Knights of Tastevin, Grand Constable and all of you, knights of the brotherhood, ladies and gentlemen, good evening!"

"First, let me tell you right away how excited I am to be here among you tonight. Could I ever have imagined that I would be crowned with such laurels within the walls of this distinguished château that has so often inspired me? As a child romping in the vineyards of the Médoc and learning to swim in the water holes of the Hourtin pond, I could not see myself playing or living in any place other than that corner of the world, where vineyards were loved with so much passion. For a long time I thought that good wines were made only there, because you know that the natives of Bordeaux are a bit chauvinist, and my grandfather never drank anything other than his own wine. I found out later that his wine was far from the best, but I must admit that for me, it still has a particular bouquet. It seems that we often pattern our lives after those first impressions of childhood.

"I like to recall that it was a child of your land, a son of Burgundy with visionary talent, who contributed to protecting the Port de la Lune from English invasions. The shores of Bordeaux owe so much to the three fortresses built by Sébastien le Prestre de Vauban. That was another time. The world may never be at peace, but wine abolished our borders long ago. I have traveled extensively in lands even farther from my culture than Burgundy, and I have learned that wine is a universal language. Each time a man raises his glass and empties it, I know what cloth he is cut from, what stuff he is made of. I can guess his disposition, sometimes his sense of humor, his reserve, his impatience or his sense of moderation, his wit or lack of tact. No need to talk further: the drinker reveals himself and sometimes shows what he would like to hide. The older I get, the more I believe that this is one of the greatest revelations of wine.

"To tell you that it is an honor to be named Chevalier du Tastevin in a setting as glorious as the Vougeot château would be a little banal and superficial. For me it's a sign of friendship more than an honorary distinction. I have too many good memories, between Côte de Nuits and Côte de Beaune, too many faithful readers and vigilant winemakers between Chalon and Mâcon, not to show my pleasure and my great joy in this moment. Finally, since I must conclude, and I promised not to talk too long, I will quote one of your own, Jean-François Bazin, who does honor to the Burgundian parlance and wrote this: 'The Confrérie des Chevaliers du Tastevin is like a ray of sunlight in the darkness of the cellars!' So this is what I say: I'm here in broad daylight, even if I incur the wrath of all my friends in Bordeaux."

§ § §

The dining room of the Hôtel de Vougeot was still empty at this early-morning hour. With his mind still reeling from alcohol, excitement, songs, and laughter, Benjamin Cooker had slept little. A cool, almost cold shower had restored his calm, and he had stretched his legs walking among the rows of vines that bordered the establishment. In keeping with an old habit, the winemaker had taken a room in the hotel's annex behind the courtyard. He was pleased with room number nine, whose window with small panes of glass opened onto the vineyards of Vougeot.

"Did you sleep well, sir?" a waitress named Aurélie asked, dipping an Earl Grey teabag into a white porcelain teapot.

"Well, let's say I closed one eye from time to time, miss."

"Did you see what happened across the street? Some kids covered the whole café with graffiti."

Cooker went to the window, parted the lace curtains, and wiped the condensation from the glass. On the facade of the Rendez-vous des Touristes, black letters were clumsily scrawled in spray paint between a wall thermometer and some empty window boxes. He squinted.

Domine exaudi orationem meam
et clamor meus ad te veniat

Cooker read the phrase in a whisper. He had studied Latin in his youth.

"It's such a shame to dirty everything that way," Aurélie grumbled, heating up the teapot. "Especially to write such nonsense."

Cooker sat down before his plate and observed the hotel employee. He had known her as a girl and suddenly realized that she had become a woman in the two years since he had last seen her. Her ruddy cheeks had become more defined, and mascara accentuated her long black eyelashes. Her hair was pulled back and showed off her forehead. The somewhat awkward and pudgy apprentice who used to hide her eyes behind long bangs was now a lovely waitress whose precise gestures and alluringly delicate nose added to her charm.

"I know it's those boys from Dijon who did it," she went on as she placed the teapot on the table.

"Are you sure?"

"Who else could it be? The neighborhoods over there are full of graffiti like that. You wouldn't believe what it's like near the train station. And what really kills me is that it's not even French. I don't understand a word of it."

"It's Latin."

"Ah, I was sure it wasn't French."

Cooker breathed in the aroma of bergamot and took several swallows, burning his tongue. He put his cup down and slipped his coat on.

"Have a nice day, Aurélie. I'll hold onto my key, because I might be getting back late."

He crossed the road and stood in front of the defaced wall of the café. The paint was dry, and only a few letters had dribbled down the yellowish stucco. He took out his notebook and wrote down the Latin phrase, taking care to translate it accurately.

Lord, hear my prayer.
Let my cry for help to reach you.

As soon as he entered the café, all conversation stopped. Cooker sat down nonchalantly at the first table and ordered an espresso. The owner brought him a small cup of very bitter coffee, which Cooker tried to sweeten with three cubes of sugar. The café patrons started talking again, but quietly and warily. Three men who looked like retirees were filling out their trifecta sheets and muttering. At the end of the bar, two young sporty types with low foreheads and protruding lower lips sipped beer and whispered to each other. They were wearing similar royal-blue tracksuits. Next to Cooker, a homely couple sat across from each other in silence; the woman, whose triple chin spilled over the collar of a knitted vest, was shooting sidelong, slightly fearful glances across the room, while her husband was picking his nose with satisfactory results.

"May I borrow your newspaper?" Cooker asked.

"Go right ahead!"

He carefully pushed aside his cup and opened *Le Bien Public* on the table. The snowstorms in the Nuits-Saint-Georges were the lead story in the paper. Cooker perused an article on local sand-blasters and the weather forecast for Easter week. On page three, he happened upon his picture, in black and white, which took up two columns.

The slightly overexposed photo, taken during his speech, made him look like a jovial and cunning horse trader at a country fair. It did not at all resemble him and made him smile, as did the article's headline: "Winemaker Cooker gets toast, is spared roast at multicourse Vougeot fête."

The couple—farmers, Cooker presumed—watched him without uttering a word. The chatter at the bar grew livelier. "They're real bastards from the city pulling that shit." Gray coils of cigarette smoke floated upward in the harsh ceiling light.

"Worse than dogs lifting their legs!"

"What do you mean, René?"

From his vantage point, Cooker could see a fine foam moustache under the nose of one of the beer drinkers.

"They write their crap like they piss against a wall!"

"Ah, I get it now."

The café owner turned on the radio. It was a nostalgic channel that seemed to crackle from beyond the grave. A duo from the seventies chirped with optimism in the sputtering of the radio.

"It's taking the cops long enough to get here, as if they had anything else to do."

Then they took out a game of dice and a green felt cloth.

"All the same, if I catch those little shits—"

Everyone counted their tokens without paying attention to the refrain, in which "Venice" rhymed with "Paris." The barely snuffed-out cigarette butts continued to smolder in the ashtrays.

"The cops?"

"Hell no. The little shits who wrote all this trash—we're gonna smash their faces in, believe me!"

Cooker turned to the couple and said, "Excuse me for interrupting. Did that happen last night?"

"The scribblings?" grumbled the old woman. "We saw them this morning. Definitely weren't there yesterday, were they, Emile?"

"Can you tell me where Vougeot's priest lives?"

"There ain't no priest in Vougeot and no church, neither."

"As a matter of fact, now that you mention it, I can't remember seeing a bell tower," Cooker said, pursing his lips. "I hadn't even paid attention."

The woman rubbed her triple chin and looked at him intently. "In Vougeot, you don't get married, and you don't die."

"That seems rather reasonable to me," Cooker smiled as he stood up. He left two euros on the table, nodded politely, and took his leave.

He walked back up the main street toward the river. Slabs of frozen snow edged the road. On the parapet of the bridge that spanned the Vouge, the same black writing ran across the cement.

Non abscondas faciem tuam a me;
in quacunque die tribulor

Cooker took out his fountain pen and jotted down the phrase before translating it.

Do not turn your face from me
In my day of trouble.

He continued walking to the small locks that constricted the river, abruptly transforming it into a narrow channel. He stopped for a moment to look at the walls on the water's edge, which were covered with thick patches of moss. Then he turned around to go to the grocery store. He bought the paper, a box of cashews, and a post-card. It was only upon leaving the store that he noticed the graffiti running the length of a low wall near the ancient washhouse.

Inclina ad me aurem tuam:
in quacunque die invocavero te,
volciter exaudi me.

Again he reached for his notebook and transcribed the phrase diligently, despite the biting cold, which was numbing his fingers.

Incline your ear to listen
When I call,
be quick to answer

A gust of wind stung his face, and he pulled his collar up to his ears. In the distance, crows squawked in the vines. Their stricken cawing dissolved in a milky sky that was so low it merged with the snow-powdered earth.

Cooker shivered.

2

The tasting had already begun when he arrived, out of breath, in the large room of Vougeot's ancient wine and spirits storehouse. The experts were seated in groups of six and moving glasses around on the tablecloths in a slow and formal ballet that seemed almost contrived. Cooker greeted everyone, apologizing for his tardiness, and went to the seat reserved for him as the Tastevinage guest of honor. He went to work immediately.

Dozens of bottles were wrapped in orange silk paper and displayed on the table between stainless-steel spittoons and wicker baskets full of rolls. Each taster had a notebook for comments. There was barely any talking. Wet swishing, tongue-clicking, and elegant gurgling were the predominant sounds rising in the crisp air of the wine warehouse.

Cooker was tired from the night before but quickly managed to concentrate. He had no trouble getting into the spirit of the game. He had prepared long and hard for it back in Bordeaux by studying the Tastevin Burgundy wine reference book. Around him, nearly two hundred fifty tasters—all elite handpicked palates—were assuming the posture of expert connoisseurs, displaying the learned gestures of acknowledged specialists. He had spotted some old acquaintances, several renowned wine growers, important wine merchants, brokers, oenologists, some researchers from the university, heads of viticulture unions, popular restaurateurs, brilliant sommeliers, and a handful of knowledgeable amateurs. Among the witnesses were local officials and personalities, as well as a well-informed assembly of specialized journalists, including several leading Parisian experts whose vitriolic writing made Michelin-star chefs tremble.

The Tastevinage session had been wonderfully well organized, and the hosts from the brotherhood were seeing to its successful unfolding without participating in the tasting. This served to guarantee neutrality. The questions posed by the jury were of devilishly simple precision: "Is this wine worthy of the appellation and vintage that appear on the label? Is it truly representative of them? Is this a wine that I would be happy to own in my cellar and proud to offer to a friend?" There were many fine points that were not to be influenced by preconceptions, moods, natural inclinations, memory lapses, or subjective reactions. Presented anonymously, each of the fifteen bottles swaddled in opaque wrapping was slapped with a concise label indicating only its appellation with no mention of the winemaker or the merchant. Cooker was enjoying the atmosphere of this ritual, which blended the sacred and the profane. All these furrowed brows gave his fellow judges the forbidding—some would say merciless—appearance of courtroom magistrates.

Cooker knew perfectly well that the stakes were high and that winemakers and the rest of the profession awaited these evaluations with a certain amount of anxiety. Initially, he tasted the small bottles fairly quickly in order to feel them in his mouth. His colleagues seemed surprised to see him proceed this way: a quick movement of the glass to make the wine speak, a swallow, and one or two swirls around the palate. Then he would spit it out immediately. Some, convinced that the famous Benjamin Cooker could do no wrong, revised their strategy and imitated him. When he had finished this preliminary trial, he took up each wine again. But this time he lingered over the visual quality, tipping his glass to better observe the transparency, the brilliance, the tint, and the intensity of the color. Then he would bring the wine to his nose to capture the whole aromatic expression in a tight bundle of details that he quickly jotted in his notebook.

After detecting the most harmonious bouquets, he swirled each wine in his mouth with exaggerated slowness, breathing in a little air to oxygenate the liquid. He closed his eyes and held himself straight in his chair while leaning his head slightly forward and putting his hands flat on the table. Then he would spit and start over without changing his posture. He analyzed the subtlest flavors, the astringencies, the delicacies of certain tannins, the powerful first impressions, the disappointing finishes, the acidity, and the roundness. From time to time, he would nibble a roll to cleanse his palate.

Fifteen swallows of red wine carefully swished and re-swished were enough for him. The dice were cast. He put aside his notebook, cracked his knuckles, gave an enormous yawn, and stood to go stretch his legs in the welcome hall. On the way, Cooker shook some hands, patted the back of some old acquaintances, brushed past quite a few people without really excusing himself, and joked with one of the knights of the Order who was observing from the back of the room. After a few moments, he returned to his seat and quickly took a small swallow of each wine without spitting. He reread his notes, crossed out two or three words, and then rose again to join the session chairman.

Seeing him proceed this way, some people lost a bit of their assurance and kept their eyes on him. Cooker felt their cautious curiosity. A number of them seemed to be losing their bearings. They wore doubtful expressions and seemed absorbed in unspoken questions. So this was how the dreaded Benjamin Cooker operated? The man who was believed to be so serious, almost ascetic, was behaving like a dilettante with an approach that would have been considered casual if he had not proven his talent.

Ultimately, one-third of the wines tasted were worthy of the coveted stamp. The award winners would have the distinguished honor of putting the famous insignia created in 1935 by the French artist Hansi—Jean-Jacques Waltz—on their bottles. The insignia was a purple shield with a small barrel at the bottom, a knight's helmet in the middle, and, at the top, a white-bearded, red-faced member of the Order of the Knights holding a cup and a bottle. A rope of green vine leaves framed the picture. Cooker did not wait for the complete announcement of the results before taking his leave. He said good-bye to the organizers and explained that he had another business meeting. He promised to stop by and see them at the offices of the Confrérie in Nuits-Saint-Georges.

As he left the château, he checked his cell phone for messages. His assistant's hoarse voice suggested some possible bad news about an Entre-Deux-Mers estate, and he called him right back.

"Virgile, what's going on?"

"Hello, boss, you don't need to worry. I solved the problem."

"Meaning?"

"I went to Sadirac myself to do the decanting, and I brought the samples back to the lab. Alexandrine will analyze them this afternoon if she has time. Otherwise, tomorrow morning at the very latest."

"Don't take advantage of her conscientiousness. Miss La Palussière is overwhelmed these days."

"No worries, sir, I know how to handle it, and, well, she accepted a lunch date."

"Bravo, Virgile. I see you are not giving up. Aside from that, how's the weather in Bordeaux?"

"Nice, as usual. I hope we'll be able to eat outside."

"Enjoy it while you can! It's awfully cold here."

"So the life of a knight is not so easy?" Virgile could not resist joking.

"It's unbearable. I just tasted some little gems, including a Morey-Saint-Denis that was quite magnificent. I am going to have to spend some more time in this region."

As he spoke, Cooker was walking toward the village, his wool scarf wrapped around his chin. He picked up his pace to get warmer, gave a few final pieces of advice to his assistant, greeted the lab director, and promised to call back the afternoon of the following day.

As he approached the grocery store, he spotted a police van parked at the corner. Uniformed men were interrogating the shopkeeper, while some of their colleagues were taking pictures of the graffiti on the bridge.

"We can't let this drag on," one of them said. "The same thing is happening in Gilly."

Cooker kept on walking as if he had not heard anything and headed for his hotel. In the distance, the massive silhouette of the Vougeot château seemed to be dozing in the middle of a burial ground of vines whose bony limbs and gnarled stumps were packed all the way to the back of the vineyard. A thick sky was brushing against the points of the towers where the crows were performing sinister and mocking spirals.

§ § §

The canvas top of Cooker's convertible was sagging slightly under the fine layer of crusty snow, and he had to scrape the windshield with the blade of a Laguiole knife that had been miraculously abandoned in the back of the trunk. It took three tries before the engine started. Cooker waited for the confident purring before getting on the road to Gilly-les-Cîteaux. Traversing the wintry Burgundy terrain in a vintage Mercedes

280SL that he had failed to have serviced only heightened Cooker's sense of adventure.

As he drove, the land became almost foreign. The highway seemed to serve as a paved border that marked the age-old conflict between the vineyards and the plowed fields, between the noble dryness of the highlands and the ordinary generosity of the lowlands. In less than ten minutes, he was in the deserted town of Gilly. He parked next to a war memorial and walked slowly around the square, where he saw scrawling on the pillar.

Quia cinerem tamquam panem manducabam
et potum meum cum fletu miscebam

He slid his hand into the inside pocket of his coat to grab his fountain pen and notebook.

Ashes are the bread I eat;
and to my drink I add my tears.

On the wall of the church, there was another message in writing that didn't seem as controlled.

A facie irae et increpationis tuae;
quia elevans allisisti me.

Cooker had more trouble translating this phrase, whose syntax seemed convoluted.

Before your anger and your fury;
since you raised me up and
then cast me aside.

Finally, he approached an old house, tastefully renovated with a respect for the materials of the era. The two large panels of the entry door had been defaced with a heavily written message.

Dieis mei sicut umbra declinaverunt,
et ego sicut foenum arui.

Some of the letters were dripping between the granular veins of the oak.

My days are like the waning shadow,
and I am like withering grass.

The writing was identical to what he had seen on the wall in Vougeot. And once again, there were only two phrases, which, put together, seemed to form a coherent stanza. It wouldn't be long before the police arrived to collect evidence and take photographs. He had to clear out as soon as possible if he did not want to run into them.

Cooker put his notebook and his fountain pen deep in his Loden jacket and then rubbed his hands and blew on them. In this country of silence and mystery, he knew only one man capable of enlightening him.

3

The road stretched before him, gentle and monotonous. There was a soothing quality about the forest surrounding the Cîteaux Abbey, filled with hornbeams and oak and beech trees. Cooker put in an old Verdi cassette. The worn-out tape made the lamenting violins sound even more sorrowful. Listening to the voice undulating between smiles and tears, he imagined this *Traviata* in the faded silk of an over-the-hill courtesan, irrevocably plagued by rapid consumption. He turned down the volume as he approached the entrance to the monastery and parked under a row of poplars.

The abbey's porter, who had a room near the entrance and had greeted many visitors over the years, welcomed Cooker warmly. Eight years earlier, the winemaker had stayed in the abbey's guest room while he was writing the first edition of his guide. On the advice of a friend from Burgundy, a winemaker in Coulanges-la-Vineuse, he had written a letter to the father superior. He was hoping to get access to the

Cistercian archives. The monks had consented to give this curious man from Bordeaux the privilege of nosing through the abbey's old papers. For more than a week, Cooker had bent willingly to the monastic discipline, attending all the prayer services, participating in the domestic chores, and spending his free time in the dark corners of the library. There, he had listened to Brother Clément, a small vivacious man of letters, whose humility was as impressive as his knowledge of the history of Burgundy. There was nothing he did not know about this complex and multilayered region marked by dynastic issues, feudal land divisions, the vagaries of commerce and wars, the parceling of vineyards, and the political strategies of the first wine traders. Without the support of Brother Clément, the manuscript would not have had such a wealth of anecdotes and details gleaned, for the most part, directly from Cîteaux's documents.

Cooker waited nearly a quarter of an hour in the entrance of the cloister. He paced, recalling how the silence and deliberate slowness he had expected were nothing like what he had found here. This meditative place had bustled with activity then, as it surely did now. Memories came flooding back to him—the echoes in the corridors, the blessings in the refectory, the bells, the thundering organ during Sunday Mass, the collective prayers, the rustling robes, the trundling tractor in the fields, and the clinking of dishes in the scullery. Although his business and family obligations absorbed him now, Cooker still thought about these Cîteaux monks. He was moved to find himself back within these thick walls, where minutes seemed to expand and make one forget that time was passing.

In the distant interplay of light and shadow, a small stooped man was approaching. He was taking baby steps, and his rail-thin body was swimming in the folds of a white robe that dragged along the flagstones. Cooker moved toward him.

"Brother Clément?"

"Have I really changed that much, Mr. Cooker?"

The winemaker immediately regretted having spoken so quickly and put out his hand in response.

"I don't blame you," the monk said and sighed, slipping his bony fingers into Benjamin's palm. "I can hardly recognize myself sometimes."

"You have grown very thin," Cooker said.

"My dear friend, one must depart light. Clean and light. The body empty and the heart clear. God is calling me, and I am ready. To tell the truth, I have never felt closer to Him."

"I envy your serenity, Brother Clément. If you weren't such a chatterbox, I'd mistake you for a holy man!"

"And you're just as sarcastic as ever," the monk said with a smile. He sat down with difficulty on the edge of a white stone bench. "Don't change a thing, and keep saying what you think. With your good manners, you can get away with it. I like that."

"I always wondered how you managed to take a vow of silence. To spend your whole life being quiet!"

"Who told you Cistercian monks took a vow a silence or, for that matter, that I spent my life being quiet?"

"That's what people imagine."

"People have strange ideas about monastic life. You know, there's no place noisier than a monastery. In fact, I remember you saying that when you were here the last time. At any rate, people imagine all sorts of things."

"True enough."

"You see, I think we live in a land of silence here at Citeaux, where a man keeps his word."

Cooker stood facing the monk. With the tip of his shoe, he played with a small pebble that had come loose from the flagstone.

"I believe some people think you are infallible," Brother Clément continued. "Everyone who reads your guide believes that it all comes very easily for you."

"As a matter of fact, no one suspects just how much work goes into the *Cooker Guide*. At any rate, it's never good to give the appearance that you've taxed yourself. You have to put on a smile, look inspired, and give the impression that it is all done with great ease and pleasure. Not many people are interested in knowing the truth."

"Funny calling that you've followed," the monk said and sighed. "I have often wondered how you manage not to get bored."

"You just need to have faith. But that's not something I'm going to be telling you about!"

Brother Clément chuckled and rubbed his hands together with a glimmer of mischief in his eyes. His gaunt cheeks looked like they had been carved out of marble by a divinely inspired sculptor. "In the seminary during my youth, I was very interested in the theater. My superiors did not look upon that kindly, but I would often sneak out to see a play. That's when I realized how much life is like a comedy. I still believe that, by the way. I read many articles by Tristan Bernard, who, as you surely know, was a big theater critic. One thing he wrote bothered me at the time and still bothers me today: 'If it's bad, it bores me, and if it's good, I'm a bore.' I always found that funny, and kind of pathetic."

"I think he also said, 'I never go to see plays that I have to talk about. It might influence me.'"

"At my age, I'm still not surrendering to boredom," Brother Clément said. "I'm open to a surprise or two. Why settle for the predictable?"

"I can't agree with that point of view," Cooker replied. "For me, what's predictable isn't necessarily boring. I test, and I have to come to an understanding by experiencing for myself, by seeing for myself, and even more so, by drinking for myself. I don't know why, but without that, it's not real for me."

"I've noticed! And what brings you here today, besides the pleasure of chatting with me, of course?"

"I've been meaning to pay you a visit, but I admit that I am here sooner than I expected. Some surprising things are happening in these parts."

"I know," the old man said as he rose painfully. "Burgundy will never cease to surprise us."

"You know about the inscriptions they found in Vougeot and Gilly?"

"What do you think? Just because we are enclosed in this abbey, that we are ignorant of the world around us? Be aware, my dear Benjamin, that nothing that touches the world is unknown to us."

"I've copied each of those phrases, and it all intrigues me," the winemaker said, handing his notebook to the monk. "I translated them as best I could."

Brother Clément went through the notes and took his time to weigh each word. He was wheezing, as if just breathing was a labor.

"You managed pretty well. It's actually quite good, aside from a few turns of phrase."

"I was surprised myself that I still remembered my Latin. I think I owe it more to my years as a child in the choir than to my high school teacher. At least it seems that way, because each time I see a Latin phrase, I can't help but smell the incense."

"In that case, I can refresh your memory." The monk smiled.

"Exactly. I was counting on you. I have the feeling that I know these passages, but their origin escapes me. And who do you think could have painted all of that on the walls?"

"That's another story! Follow me."

They walked through the rhythmic shadows of the cloister before slipping under an entryway and following a dark corridor where a few rays of vapid light were trying to pierce the frosty stained-glass windows. Then they stepped through a small secret door and crossed a nearly empty room furnished with only a writing desk. Another door led to an antechamber that was just as deserted, and they finally came to the abbey library. The entire time, they did not speak a word. Brother Clément was walking slowly, forcing himself to control the wheezing and coughing fits that assailed him.

"I am moved to find myself here again," Cooker said, raising his blue-gray eyes toward the high shelves. "I have nothing but fond memories of this place."

The monk did not respond but turned toward the shelves containing hundreds of works bound in cracked leather, bundles of tied-up documents, and volumes of canon law probably no longer consulted. A fine film of dust rose up as the two men passed. Cooker felt rooted in centuries of history and timeless knowledge. At one corner of the maze, Brother Clément pulled from the stack the *Breviarium Monasticum* published in 1892 under the guidance of Father Paul Delatte from the Abbey Saint-Pierre de Solesmes. He placed the massive volume on a stand, paged through it quickly, and stopped at page ninety-four. He ran his index finger slowly down the page.

"Psalm 101 from the Book of David. This text is often called 'Prayer in times of misfortune.' It's in fact the prayer of an afflicted person who has grown weak and is pouring out a lament before the Lord. The psalm is very well known and is often quoted, too. I am surprised that you didn't remember it."

"I have lapses, Brother Clément. I don't mind admitting it. And it's been quite a while since I have immersed myself in the Bible."

"Sometimes the psalm is referred to as Psalm 102, especially in the Hebrew Bible, which predates the Greek Bible and the Vulgate by centuries. Let's look at the *New Jerusalem Bible*, which most Catholics use today, where it's Psalm 102."

Cooker leaned over the narrow table to get a better look at the opened volumes. He put on his reading glasses and knit his brows.

"Indeed, my translation is not so bad," he said without hiding a certain satisfaction.

"It's well done. You did not suffer in vain on the school benches. The phrases you copied down in Vougeot correspond to the first verse of the psalm, and the ones from Gilly correspond to the fourth."

"That could mean that two are missing. They might be scribbled on some other walls. Who knows? Maybe in another village."

"Not necessarily. Maybe they were deliberately omitted."

> For my days are vanishing like smoke,
> my bones burning like an oven;
> like grass struck by blight, my heart is
> withering,
> I forget to eat my meals.
> From the effort of voicing my groans
> my bones stick out through my skin.

Brother Clement whistled with excitement. "Read the next part. Very interesting."

> I am like a desert-owl in the wastes,
> a screech-owl among ruins,
> I keep vigil and moan
> like a lone bird on a roof.
> All day long my enemies taunt me,
> those who once praised me
> now use me as a curse.

Leaning over the monk's shoulder, Cooker read the words in a low voice. His lips were hardly moving, as if he were praying and absorbed in the soothing rhythm of the chant.

"There you go. This is the passage that intrigues me the most," the monk said, straightening up with difficulty.

"This one?" Cooker asked. "Why a desert owl?"

"I suppose you wouldn't have those in your native England," the monk responded with amusement.

"I would have just translated that as a pelican." The winemaker shrugged.

"That would not necessarily have been wrong. In medieval Europe, the pelican was thought to be particularly attentive to her young, to the point of providing her own blood by opening up her breast when no other food was available. Pelican or owl, that doesn't change the problem."

"I don't know what to make of all this," Cooker confessed in a vexed tone. "Why would someone be covering walls with verses from a psalm?"

"Maybe it should be seen as a plea, a way of addressing God or man. I don't know. This is about someone who surely has serious reasons to complain."

"Still, there are other ways to express your feelings."

"It seems all our big cities are covered with graffiti," the monk said between coughs. "Some people see it as a youthful protest, a cry for help, or even a cry of desperation. Some of it is even considered art. These days, people can find very absurd ways to express their discontent."

"It's true that the method, writing with spray paint, makes it seem similar to other vandalism, except the author knows Latin and refers to the Old Testament. You must agree, it is somewhat unusual."

"I don't know what to say, Benjamin. You'd have to study the text in order to decipher the code and uncover the hidden meaning. There must be one. At least I hope there is. In the body of the Psalter you find everything and its opposite: threats, confessions of sin, petitions, vows of chastity, grievances, gratitude—everything."

"You're right. You'd need to deconstruct this psalm in order to—"

"Take this. It's a gift," the monk interrupted, handing him a hardback fabric-covered *New Jerusalem Bible.* "I suppose you don't have one with you, since you're traveling."

"No, I don't, I confess."

"In that case, your penance will be to reread certain passages, even if it means you fall asleep doing so!"

The two men promised to see each other before the winemaker left town. Brother Clément stayed in the library, citing overdue research as an excuse, and did not offer to walk his visitor to the door. But he did point Cooker to a secret passage to use as a shortcut.

As soon as Cooker was outside the abbey, he took a deep breath and strolled among the poplars. Then he slid behind the wheel of his convertible and sat quietly, as though protected by the fog of condensation on the car windows. With his hands on the steering wheel, his eyes half-closed, and his lips moving over the verses of the psalm, he dwelled on the powerless lamentations. At last he took out his cell phone and pressed the contact button, where his assistant's number was on his list of favorites.

"Hello, Virgile?"

"Yes, boss. Is something wrong?"

"Why do you ask?"

"You told me you would call tomorrow afternoon. I am surprised to hear from you so soon."

"Do you know Burgundy, Virgile?"

"Not really, boss. Not at all, in fact. Just what I've read in books."

"Okay, then come and get a taste of it," Cooker said. "I'll expect you tomorrow."

"How do I get there?"

"Figure it out. Ask my secretary to get you a ticket."

"By train? I'll have to route through Paris. That's a long way, boss!"

"And stop calling me 'boss.' You know how much that irritates me."

"Yes, bo... uh, sir!"

4

He was dressed in a fine linen tunic and had Roman sandals on his feet as he climbed Mount Sinai on the back of a mule. Two shots rang out. In the distance, the half-nude Jesus, a chastely veiled Mary Magdalene, the faithful Emmaus, and half a dozen apostles were assembled in the shelter of an olive tree. The violent echo of the explosions faded into the night.

Cooker sat up suddenly in his bed, felt around for the light switch, and knocked the Bible off the night table. Outside, he could hear shutters banging open and several piercing screams.

Wearing a bathrobe made of wool from the Pyrenees and a pair of kidskin slippers, he walked down the steps of the annex, crossed the courtyard, and found himself on the main road of Vougeot. A group of villagers were gathered a few feet from the post office. An elderly man with a moustache was yelling from a window and brandishing a hunting rifle.

"Don't mess with the Mancenot brothers! Don't mess with us!"

Cooker cautiously approached the circle of people gathered on the sidewalk. He recognized the woman with the triple chin and her husband, as well as the owner of the Rendez-vous des Touristes, who was kneeling by a body. A rather lost-looking woman stood apart from another group of people he didn't know, all motionless in the freezing wind.

"Go get a blanket!" a small bald man shouted to a young girl with a frightened expression. "The checkered one at the back of the linen closet! Hurry!"

Cooker drew closer. A boy was lying on the asphalt, his body curled on its right side, his eyes rolled upward, legs twitching and trembling. Blood from his abdomen was streaming slowly through his jacket. The steady flow was beginning to form a thick shiny puddle on the pavement.

"He's done for, the little bastard!" the man with the moustache continued to yell, shaking his rifle.

"Have you called an ambulance?" Cooker asked as he leaned over the injured boy.

"Yes! They are coming from Nuits-Saint-George!" someone answered.

"It's better not to move him," one of the women said as she averted her eyes.

"Goddammit, is that blanket coming or not?"

"What happened?" Cooker asked, pulling his bathrobe tighter.

"One of the Mancenot brothers fired," replied the café owner. "It's that moron, Ernest!"

The man with the gun was still standing in the frame of the window, his weapon at arm's length. He had the crimson face and bewildered look of lonely old men who drown their celibacy in cheap liquor and hatred of the world. Behind him, a furtive silhouette was pacing under the halo of a bare lightbulb.

"And Honoré does not dare show his face. Look at that!" shouted the fat woman's husband.

"That's the end of them pissing us off, those assholes!" the shooter yelled, sticking out his chest. "Two buckshots full blast. I didn't miss!"

"Shut your mouth, Ernest!" the café owner yelled, his jaw tense.

Then Cooker saw another body lying a few yards away from the group. He approached the second victim, whose left cheek had been blown away by the volley of lead. The other side of his face was intact, his open eye looking dazed. The kid could hardly have been eighteen. His long hair was soaking in a bloody pile of flesh and bone shards. No one else dared to look at him. He was lying there, his head mangled, abandoned to the cold and wind. Cooker suppressed a gasp of disgust.

The girl arrived with the checkered blanket. Someone grabbed it to cover the boy whose blood continued to pool on the pavement. His legs were shaking faster and faster; a red dribble was beginning to flow from his nose.

Cooker heard the wail of sirens. An ambulance with a flashing blue light turned from the highway to cross the bridge and was speeding toward them. It was closely followed by a police car. Everyone moved aside when the paramedics and police officers leaped from their vehicles. Ernest Mancenot had disappeared from the window. The police officers walked around the victims without hiding their revulsion. The paramedics quickly decided to transport the wounded boy to the hospital in Dijon and to call for a second ambulance to take the dead boy to the medical examiner's office. They carefully slipped the curled-up boy, his legs still shaking, onto a stretcher. As the speeding ambulance disappeared, the police officers started questioning members of the crowd.

The café owner spoke up and explained briefly that the two boys had been shot down by one of the Mancenot brothers while they were getting ready to spray paint the wall of the post office. Cooker turned and then saw the black inscription on the facade, near the mailbox: "In V..." in round, thick letters. The victims had not had the time to write any more than that. Old Ernest had shot them down in the middle of the act. The can of spray paint had rolled into the gutter. An officer recovered it and wrapped it in a plastic bag.

"Do you know the victims?" the captain inquired.

"Cedric and David Bravart, two cousins," replied the woman with the triple chin. "One of them is from Vougeot, and the other is from Gilly. That one there is David."

The policeman glanced at the body, frowned, and raised his head in the direction of the window, where Ernest was now standing again.

"Mr. Mancenot! Put down your gun, and get out here!"

"I did my job!" the old man barked.

"I am waiting for you, sir! Do not make us come and get you!"

All eyes were focused on the Mancenot brothers' house, an austere and charmless building weighed down by its granular and graying stucco. Minutes ticked by. The police officers were waiting near the entrance. Cooker sneezed and crossed his arms to warm himself. His feet were freezing. He was thinking about going back to the hotel and putting on something warmer when the Mancenot brothers stuck their drunken faces through the half-open door. Ernest spat on the ground and looked around defiantly.

"Two cartridges, two targets! Gotta have balls, that's all!"

He was summarily handcuffed and pushed into the police cruiser, while Honoré, looking even more stunned than his brother, began to whimper. "Don't worry, Ernest. I'll take care of everything."

While a police officer went upstairs to recover the gun and the cartridge cases, the second ambulance arrived, just ahead of a rattling Citroen 2CV. Out of this climbed a man in his fifties with salt-and-pepper hair in a ponytail. He was wearing a mauve scarf and had a camera around his neck. A reporter from *Le Bien Public*. He snapped a few photos of the stretcher as it was sliding into the van, the Mancenot's still-open window, and the graffiti just barely begun. Then he questioned several of the bystanders he seemed to know well. Each one gave him more or less the same version of the story, some of them reveling in describing the state of the bodies in minute detail and reporting the old man's deranged behavior.

Cooker was about to return to his room when he heard a man call out, "Mr. Cooker?"

The winemaker jumped and turned to see who was talking to him. "To whom do I owe the pleasure? Do we know each other?"

"Well, I know you," the man responded. "My name is Bressel, I wrote the article on your induction into the brotherhood of the Chevaliers du Tastevin."

"Ah, so you're the one."

If the moment had not been so tragic, Cooker would have smiled and commented on the ridiculous headline and unflattering photo.

"Yes, I'm the one who covered the Chapter of the Tulips," Robert Bressel confirmed. "Do you intend to stay in the region for long?"

"I don't know. Why?"

"I'd love to do an interview."

"I'm supposed to leave in four or five days."

"It would be great to have the opinion of an expert like yourself on the latest Tastevinage."

Shivering, Cooker suddenly realized the incongruity of the situation. Here he was, standing in the middle of the street at five in the morning, in pajamas, bathrobe, and slippers.

"Maybe this is not the best time to discuss this," he said, holding back a sneeze. "I need to get some more sleep."

"I live in Saint-Bernard," Bressel insisted. "Last house on the way out of town. You can't miss it. If you feel like it and have the time, stop by and see me."

"I'll think about it, sir."

Cooker nodded a good-bye and walked quickly toward the hotel annex. Once in his room, he ran a scalding hot bath and soaked in it for more than an hour while reading the first thirty Psalms of David.

§ § §

A waft of patchouli incense assailed his nostrils even before he had crossed the threshold. Cooker wiped the soles of his Lobbs on the horsehair doormat, took in one last lungful of fresh air, and dove into the vestibule. Dozens of little candles twinkled on a shelf that ran all along the wall and seemed to come alive under the haunting undulations of an Indian sitar.

Robert Bressel offered him a cup of green tea and invited him to sit in a heap of cushions with batik covers that looked particularly uncomfortable. The winemaker preferred a carved African stool. Several naively sculpted snakes were crawling along its base. The living room was rather large, but the motley decor devoured the space. Cooker's eyes widened at the dozens of bouquets of dried flowers, numerous oriental knickknacks, terra-cotta reproductions of Aztec gods, ivy dripping from macramé suspensions, an enormous plastic elephant painted gold, tourist posters of Sumatra tacked on the walls among yellowed posters of Che Guevara, Jimi Hendrix, and Romy Schneider, a Balinese armoire, a yellow-straw Mexican hat, a Napoleon III–era china cabinet, precariously stacked books, CDs strewn everywhere, a copper bowl full of moldy cereal, and a laptop on the floor, which was covered with oriental rugs and hemp mats. The sinuous sitar music irritated Cooker's auditory passages.

The journalist poured the tea in Chinese cups while imitating the sweeping ethereal gestures of North African Tuaregs. The mauve scarf knotted around his blond hair was hanging over a mohair sweater that bore a geometric pattern of lamas. He sniffed his cup and raised his eyes toward the ceiling.

"It's a gyokuro from Japan. The best!"

"Thank you very much," Cooker said politely from his Congolese stool.

"I prefer it to the bancha from China, which is too fibrous, and the oolong from Taiwan, which is too pale."

"I tend to stick with Grand Yunnan, like my father. Or else I make do with any Earl Grey or Darjeeling."

"It's true that it's the national drink in England," Bressel said. Cooker noted that Bressel looked a bit disappointed by his placid ignorance of fine teas.

"Yes, I drink almost as much tea as wine. That tells you how hopelessly Franco-British I am!"

"Speaking of which, I need some biographical information for a note at the beginning of the interview."

"My secretary will send you a whole press kit," Cooker said, cutting him short. He didn't care to expand any more on his personal history.

They spoke quietly, mostly about wine production. Slumped in his pile of cushions, Robert Bressel did not have a tape recorder for the interview, but instead used a big spiral notebook. Cooker gave his cautious opinion on the samples he had had the honor to taste at the Château du Clos de Vougeot. Of the eight hundred and nineteen wines from the 2000, 2001, and 2002 vintages, he admitted that he had tasted only a dozen. But the experience of the Tastevinage had convinced him that he needed to spend part of his visit in the Morey-Saint-Denis area, which he regarded as one of the finest terroirs of the world.

"No kidding?" the reporter marveled.

"I rarely joke when I'm talking about wine, unless I've drunk too much of it, which, of course, is a hazard of the trade."

The interview continued in a more or less relaxed, almost friendly tone. The sitar had ceased its soporific whirling, and Cooker poured himself a second cup of green tea. He expounded on the state of the wine business, the problems of exportation, the specificity of pinot noir—the flagship of the Burgundy grape varietals—the need to age the best wines and the care exercised in decanting, the unfairly underrated communal appellations, the heterogeneous nature of the wine-growing region of the hautes-côtes, climatic variations, the parceling of terrain, the rising values of the Mâconnais, and the new decrees of the agricultural regulatory agency INAO. After all that, Cooker could not resist the urge to ask a few questions of his own. He had talked enough about wines and the wine business. Before the interview ended, he intended to steer the discussion toward other things that were on his mind.

"And I must also say that there is no lack of excitement in the area," he ventured.

"Do you mean what happened last night?"

"Since my arrival, some very disturbing things have occurred. This graffiti on the walls, the two kids who were shot. Usually this region is rather peaceful and—"

"Pardon me for contradicting you, but Burgundy has never been a peaceful place. Admittedly, it's a good life, and I agree that people envy the apparent tranquility, but that's not the whole picture."

"Oh, really? What are you trying to say?" Cooker asked as he poured himself a third cup of tea.

"I wasn't really surprised to see that graffiti yesterday morning."

"Were you expecting it?"

"Not at all. I just think it is one more mystery among so many others here," Bressel said.

"A rather quickly solved mystery at that, mind you."

"Frankly, I find it hard to believe that the two kids could have scrawled those inscriptions, especially in Latin!"

"And yet they were interrupted while spray painting the walls."

"So? What does that prove?"

"Not much, really," Cooker said. "Have you heard anything about the injured kid?"

"He died around eight o'clock at the hospital in Dijon. I found out just as you were arriving."

"That's awful," Cooker sighed.

"Absolutely horrible. Ernest Mancenot is in custody now, but he may very well be released on his own recognizance. He had a .10 blood-alcohol level."

"That didn't keep him from shooting straight," the winemaker said without a hint of sarcasm.

"They're a family of hunters. The two brothers are old hardened boys who have nothing else to do but hunt down game, go mushroom picking, and spend their pensions on booze."

"What kind of work did they do, exactly?"

"They drove trucks for a construction company."

"And the two kids?"

"The Bravart cousins? I think they were still in high school or maybe apprentices. To tell you the truth, I don't know much about them. I should find out. But in my opinion, they were not scholars. I know the parents a little. I wouldn't think that the Bravart household read much of the Psalms of David. People would know."

"Psalms of David, you say?" Benjamin was good at feigning surprise.

"Yes, Mister Cooker, it's about two verses from Psalm 101 or 102, depending on which Bible you consult. I learned this from my nephew, Pierre-Jean, who's a librarian in Dijon."

"You don't think the Bravart boys would have been familiar with it?"

"As I said, I wouldn't think so. But who knows? And if they were familiar with that particular psalm, you would have to wonder what their motivation was, and what the texts actually mean."

"That's my opinion, too," the winemaker said, "But now that they are dead, we'll never know what they wanted to tell us."

Robert Bressel slid over his raft of multicolored cushions and made his way slowly to the stereo. The sitar resumed its moaning. Benjamin Cooker decided it was time to leave.

5

The clock struck noon. The station was almost empty when the train from Paris came to a stop on track two. Virgile jumped down from the car with his bag over his shoulder, his sunglasses pushed up on his head, and his jacket open over a fine linen shirt. He had a radiant and always-a-bit arrogant look that young men from the southwest of France have when they cross north of the boundary line drawn by the Loire River.

"You look good," Cooker said, shaking his hand.

"I am in great shape, sir. I slept the whole trip."

"So much the better. I intend to take you on a tour of the grand dukes."

"The Dukes of Burgundy?"

"You hit the nail on the head, my boy."

As they left Dijon, the winemaker decided on going the back way and took Highway 122. He followed the signs for the Route des Grands Crus and drove slowly, enjoying the purring of the six cylinders. As they passed through the winemaking villages, Cooker cheerfully narrated without ever adopting the pedantic tone that sometimes annoyed his young assistant. They went through Chenôve, Marsannay-la-Côte, Couchey, Fixin, Brochon, Gevrey-Chambertin, Morey-Saint-Denis, Chambolle-Musigny, and finally Vougeot, which they reached an hour later, even though the most direct roads would have taken them there in no more than twenty minutes.

"It is really so different from the Bordeaux region," Virgile declared as he got out of the convertible. "Little convoluted parcels of land, no chocolate-box châteaux every hundred yards, good solid farmhouses. It smells of the earth here!"

"It is very different," Cooker said. "I thought it would be good for you to experience this terroir for yourself. Traveling can be an excellent education for young people. Besides, my grandmother always used to say: 'A change of pastures fattens the calf!'"

"Thank you for taking the trouble," the assistant said as he buttoned up his jacket and rubbed his hands together to warm them. "And to think that yesterday I was eating outside. Honestly, it's beautiful here, but you freeze your butt off."

"That's also part of the charm." Cooker smiled. "I don't think those sunglasses are going to be very useful."

They dropped Virgile's bag off in the room reserved for him in the annex, which was across from Cooker's.

"You're spoiling me, sir, with this view of the vineyards and the Clos de Vougeot château!"

They both stood at the window, arms crossed, gazing over the ocean of grapevines where the silvery sparkling of the trellises met with the milky luminescence of the sky. The field hands, in groups of three and four, were bending over the rows, straightening the wooden stakes, and stretching wires to attach the branches. Others were burning armfuls of vine shoots pruned over the winter. The plumes of white smoke skimmed the earth, refusing to rise. Pointing toward the horizon, Cooker launched into a long history of the Clos de Vougeot that Virgile found fascinating.

The centuries filed by with a richness of detail and anecdotes reminiscent of alter candles and ancient parchment. Cooker enjoyed telling Virgile about the monks from Molesmes who founded the Cîteaux Abbey on the marshy grounds where nothing grew but thin reeds known as *cîteaux*. Then he described the rock quarries not far from the hamlet of Vooget, where the first acres of vines were planted at the very beginning of the twelfth century. He recounted the rivalry with the monks of Saint-Germain, who settled in Gilly, the successive land acquisitions, the donations from the lords, and the protection by those in power. He spent time explaining the construction of the Clos de Vougeot château in 1551 by the abbot of Cîteaux, Dom Loisier, who had to stand up to his

Cistercian brothers because they criticized him for squandering God Almighty's funds.

"I won't go into the seizure of the château during the revolutionary period and all of the buybacks and shady financial negotiations, and how it was made into a hospital at the beginning of the Second World War, and the terrible explosion under the German occupation, which damaged the roof. Not to mention the fact that the four magnificent wine presses almost ended up as firewood. The Americans also requisitioned it to house prisoners after the Liberation, before the Confrérie des Chevaliers du Tastevin became the proprietors and undertook the restoration of the buildings. You see, Virgile, what fascinates me the most in all this history is the permanence of the traditions and the winemakers' attachment to this unique piece of land, their fierce protection of the appellation, and the level of quality, along with superior wine-making standards and the manual harvesting. And then there's the unalterable boundary of the terroir."

"It hasn't changed since the twelfth century?" Virgile interrupted.

"It's difficult to push back stone outer walls. The vineyard covers exactly fifty hectares, ninety-five ares, and seventy-six centiares, which makes upwards of one hundred and twenty-seven point two acres."

"I admire your precision, sir," Virgile said with a touch of impertinence.

"Make fun if you like, my boy. I am always careful to leave nothing to chance, as Francois Mauriac wrote."

"And how many people own the Clos de Vougeot?"

"About eighty sharing a hundred parcels with sixty different vinifications."

"When you say about eighty, would that be more or a bit less?"

"Well done, Virgile. You've caught me. I don't have the exact number in my head anymore. It changes, depending on sales and divisions that take place when parcels are inherited. On the other hand, I can tell you that the vineyard produces about two hundred tons of grapes, and from that, depending on the year, two hundred and fifty thousand to three hundred thousand bottles."

"And is their quality equal?"

"Not really. The nature of the terrain obviously has a determining influence, as you would suspect. The vineyard has a gradient of just three to four percent, but that is enough to create important differences. In the upper section that you see back there, the ground is stony, mainly limestone. Toward the middle, the loose layer of earth becomes somewhat thick and dense. At the bottom, the pluvial erosion has accumulated sediments, and because the constant moisture results in a thick silt, they have to drain it sometimes."

"It's true. It's fairly flat toward the lower part, and I bet that the contour of the highway, which is a bit elevated, didn't help things."

"Bravo, Virgile. Very good deduction. The water table is not far from the surface in this spot, and it tends to hold more water. Then the construction of the highway exacerbated the problem by interfering with natural drainage. If only the civil engineers had your down-to-earth common sense!"

"If I understand everything you've told me, it is rare in these parts to have this type of château in the middle of a vineyard."

"Yes, it's kind of like something you might see in Bordeaux, but the Burgundians don't do that sort of thing. They don't ruin estates. They disturb the least area possible. The vineyard is king here, and you do not dominate it with ostentatious structures."

Cooker turned away from the window and went to his own room to get a woolen scarf he had forgotten to take with him in the morning.

"Okay, let's not dawdle, Virgile. I have other things to show you."

They climbed into the convertible and got back on the highway toward Nuits-Saint-Georges. Cooker apologized for not having offered his assistant something to eat.

"Don't worry, I had a sandwich on the train that made the trip worthwhile: tasteless ham on crumbly white bread, barely fresh butter, and a jungle-rot pickle! The worst of it is that, well, I'm a bit ashamed to admit it, but I was so hungry, I thought it was delicious!"

"Those are the guilty pleasures you should not deny yourself, my dear Virgile," Cooker replied, holding back a laugh. "You know as I do that there are wines you talk about and wines you drink. They are not always one and the same."

They quickly passed through the center of Nuits-Saint-Georges and continued on toward Beaune. They decided that Virgile would visit the Hospices de Beaune, a former hospital for the poor and needy that was now a museum, while his boss would spend that time digging up research at the Athenaeum Bookstore across the way on the Rue de l'Hôtel-Dieu. They looked at their watches and agreed to give each other an hour before meeting in front of the bookstore.

Cooker rummaged with pleasure through the shelves devoted to wine. They were arranged on a platform, as if a certain homage needed to be paid to the subject. He felt at home in this bookstore that honored his profession and where one could unearth everything published on the topic. He consulted a good number of oenology treatises, monographs on cooperage, technical publications in English, historical essays, several photo albums on Burgundy, and some guide-books written by competitors with whom he often disagreed but whose expertise and convictions he respected. He foraged for nearly an hour and decided to buy the latest issue of the magazine *Burgundy Today*, whose main article was devoted to the rankings of the premiers crus, as well as half a dozen works by Pierre Poupon, including *A Taster's New Thoughts*, *The Fruits of Autumn*, *The Wine of Memories*, *Pleasures of Tasting*, *My Literary Tastings*, *The End of a Vintage*, and *The Vintner's Gospel*. Flipping through the pages, Cooker was struck by the poetry, irony, and erudition—there was, in these little well-crafted books, a spiritual vision of the vine and wine that he could not resist. A winemaker capable of expressing himself with such style was certainly an authentic writer. This Burgundian had as much talent as, or perhaps even more than, certain stunted writers of the Académie Française. One passage made him chuckle: "Smell, sniff, inhale—nothing that is fragrant or that stinks should leave you indifferent. Let odors lead you by the nose." Cooker would gladly use it in the introduction to the next edition of his guide.

He looked forward to delving into these simple yet lyrical pages that very night. He had noticed a particularly intriguing paragraph: "Thus, 'good news' was gradually revealed to me. A gospel intended for the winemaker is written in my heart. This Bible is open to all. Everyone can enter it, not just to gather the grapes left over after the harvest, but to harvest according to his thirst."

§ § §

"Magnificent, sir! It's really worth a look! I hope I wasn't too long?" Virgile had never learned to hide his enthusiasm, and that was one of his greatest qualities. He was clearly affected by his visit to the former hospital, where the sisters of the Hospices de Beaune had once cared for the destitute in a magnificent facility that featured a religious polyptych painted by Flemish artist Roger Van de Weyden. Virgile had come away talkative and excited.

"You know that I don't believe all that Holy Cross, Virgin Mary, relics, and Bible-thumping crap. But frankly, things done in the name of God are really impressive, especially when it comes to helping the poor and caring for the sick. It's great, I admit. And the roofing with the colored tiles is unbelievable. The altarpiece, too, is really superb."

"I'm happy that you liked it," Cooker said, amused by his assistant's contagious good mood.

"It's even very moving to see all those little beds lined up. I felt like I was crossing into another world. It wasn't difficult to imagine the sick coughing, crying, and being afraid to die or the nuns who served the meals, applied the bandages, and came by with spittoons. It must have been a hell of a place."

"Not necessarily. Maybe it was a place where people could be at peace and die in the loving embrace of the Lord, or at least under His watchful gaze."

"To listen to you, you'd think that God was present in all things here on earth."

"Precisely. By the way, I have some interesting things to tell you."

On the way back, the winemaker related the events of the two previous days. He summed up the matter of the psalms and told Virgile about his reunion with Brother Clément, his interview with Robert Bressel, and the slaying of the two cousins by old Mr. Mancenot. He omitted the gory details.

"That's pretty wild," Virgile said and sighed, a bit alarmed. "It doesn't surprise me that you found yourself in the middle of such a story. I would even say—no offense—that it's just like you."

"You're right in a way." Cooker smiled. "I won't deny that I sometimes have the feeling that this mystery was written for me."

Near Nuits-Saint-Geoges, Cooker turned right and headed toward Argencourt. They left Highway 74 behind them. Fine layers of sand spread over the icy frost were slowly turning the road into long tracks of mud.

After a few miles in the gloomy plains, the massive silhouette of the Cîteaux Abbey appeared in the distance.

"Does the history lesson continue?" Virgile asked in a slightly mocking tone.

"In a certain way."

The abbey porter had them wait in a parlor with bare walls, a bench, and three chairs. A crucifix watched over them. When Brother Clément came into the room, Cooker tried his best to hide his concern and sorrow. The monk was deteriorating by the hour, and he was walking even more slowly than he had the night before. There were shadows in his gaunt cheeks, and the curve of his back was more visible than ever. When he greeted them, the sound of his voice still had all of its clarity, but the resonance was frail.

"I've been thinking over this business of the psalms quite a lot, Mr. Cooker."

Virgile was silent. He looked impressed by the austere setting and this small exhausted man whose piercing gaze transfixed him.

"Well, I've reread the text many times and haven't deduced much," Cooker admitted with a sigh.

"And yet there must be some important hidden elements. The psalm is both obvious and enigmatic. Anyone can find what he wants in it and understand what suits him. But it's impossible to discern how this psalm relates to the two poor boys who were killed last night."

"You've already heard?"

"One would have to be deaf not to hear what is said in these parts."

"I have trouble believing that two kids barely eighteen years old would be amusing themselves by scrawling Latin sentences all over the walls of their towns!"

"Who knows? You must never jump to conclusions," Brother Clément suggested wisely. "But using the Old Testament to tell everyone that you are suffering is something that comes from another era!"

"They might have been taking advantage of the situation to add fuel to the fire, if only to frighten or irritate the townspeople. Perhaps they wanted to liven things up a bit."

"A type of game? It's possible. There's not much going on around here in the winter. The young people get bored."

Virgile was quiet and stood off to the side. He wasn't missing a word, but he seemed not to dare face the sharp gaze of the monk, who looked at him from time to time.

"They had started to paint some letters," Cooker continued. "But we can't know for sure what they planned to—"

"They managed to write 'In V.' Is that correct?"

"Yes, just three letters."

"We don't need to look too far: it must be the beginning of the saying '*In vino veritas.*'"

"What an idiot I am. I should have thought of that!" Cooker said, hitting his forehead with the palm of his hand.

"Provided, of course, that they knew some snippets of Latin," Brother Clément pointed out. "But the saying is pretty well known, after all."

"That's a theory that could hold water," the winemaker said. "You wouldn't have to be a Latin scholar. The Bravart cousins must have gone to Sunday school and were probably in the children's choir."

"What intrigues me even more is the time frame. The first writings were found on Wednesday, April sixth, and here we are in the middle of Holy Week, between Palm Sunday and Easter. Next Wednesday is the feast of Saint George, who is a very special martyr in Côtes-de-Nuits."

"I know, but what is the connection?"

"None, for sure. I'm asking questions. That's all. Etymologically, *George* means laborer. But the derivation isn't Latin. It's Greek. The word is composed of *gé*, the earth, and *ergon*, worker. So he is considered the patron saint of those who live by working the earth. But I digress, certainly."

Brother Clément was having increasingly more trouble enunciating. His voice was growing weaker, and his body was curling up, as if shriveling in pain. Cooker apologized for having come at such a late hour and suggested returning the following day.

"Don't worry. We've already sung vespers, and it's not yet time for evening prayer. I have all of eternity before me to rest."

"I wouldn't want to overstay my visit," Cooker said, throwing his coat over his shoulder to show they were going to leave. "Promise me that you will take it easy, Brother Clément, and don't concern yourself about this story."

"As you wish, my friend. But think about re-reading a very interesting passage from the Book of Isaiah. It's in chapter five. I know you will appreciate it."

They took their leave as night was beginning to fall, plunging the parlor into twilight. The monk said good night with a slight nod of the head. He asked the abbey porter to give him a few minutes before accompanying him to his room. The conversation had visibly exhausted him.

Cooker and Virgile got back on the road to Vougeot without feeling the need to discuss their visit. *La Traviata* accompanied them softly in an *addio del passato* that the heartbreaking voice of Maria Callas rendered even more sorrowful each time Cooker played it. The 1953 version on a cassette in pitiful condition was so moving, it drew tears of compassion for the glory and misery of courtesans.

"Don't you have anything more cheerful?" asked Virgile.

"You're right. Maybe it's not music we need," Cooker said, turning down the volume. "Come on, let's get back on track. I think I know just the thing."

Cooker passed by the sign for Vougeot, took the road to Morey-Saint-Denis, and parked in the lot of the restaurant Castel de Très Girard so that they could fittingly celebrate Virgile's first day in Burgundy. As soon as they were seated in studded armchairs in the main dining room, they opted for the gourmet menu, which included appetizer, first course, main course, cheese, and dessert. Cooker ordered smoked salmon cannelloni in lime-flavored mascarpone on a vegetable aspic and artichoke mousse, then shrimp ravioli on a bed of fennel in chervil broth, followed by stuffed saddle of rabbit in prunes covered with bacon on a bed of spinach and tomato comfit. Overwhelmed by the variety of the menu, Virgile finally chose the same dishes as his boss.

They ate more than they should have, calmly sipping a bottle of 1995 Gevrey-Chambertin from the Domaine Trapet Père et Fils. With a weary gesture they declined the cheese platter, but when the waiter offered the dessert menu, Cooker couldn't resist a pyramid of red fruit in gewurztraminer with peach sorbet, a wafer, and a sweet almond sauce. His assistant gave in to a chocolate macaroon with vanilla ice cream and a cocoa-bean emulsion.

While waiting for coffee, Cooker carefully took a Montecristo double corona from his cigar case. He rolled the flexible, well-veined tobacco-leaf wrapping between his fingers and then pulled out his little chrome guillotine. He took the time to prepare his vitole before lighting it. He discretely loosened his belt one notch, stretched his legs, leaned his head back on his chair, and, with relish, exhaled a thick puff of smoke toward the ceiling light.

"You may not believe me, Virgile, but this is the first Havana that I've smoked since I've been here."

"It's about time I got here, then!"

6

As soon as he awoke, Cooker dropped two ant-acid tablets into a glass of water, dragged himself to the shower, and stayed under its tepid spray for a good quarter of an hour. Then he gave himself a generous splash of Hermes men's cologne and slipped on a pair of wide-ribbed corduroy pants, a beige flannel shirt, and his comfortable tweed jacket, whose pockets were beginning to lose their shape a bit. He didn't have the energy to polish his Lobb country shoes while he waited for Virgile, who would certainly be a little late. Instead, he decided to consult the Bible passage that Brother Clément had referred to. He quickly found the Prophesies of Isaiah at the front of the Book of the Prophets. He briefly looked over the first pages before stopping at chapter five, verses one through seven, "The song of the vine."

> Let me sing my beloved the song of my friend for his vineyard. My beloved had a vineyard on a fertile hillside.

He dug it, cleared it of stones, and
planted it with red grapes. In the middle he built a tower, he hewed a press
there too. He expected it to yield fine
grapes: wild grapes were all it yielded.

And now, citizens of Jerusalem and
people of Judah, I ask you to judge
between me and my vineyard.

 What more could I have done for
my vineyard that I have not done?
Why, when I expected it to yield fine
grapes, has it yielded wild ones?

Someone knocked at the door. Three short
raps. Cooker went to answer it, the Bible open in
his hand.
 "Hello, sir. Sleep okay?"
 "Listen to this, Virgile," Cooker said, and read
him the passage.

Very well, I shall tell you what I am going
to do to my vineyard: I shall take away its
hedge, for it to be grazed on, and knock
down its wall, for it to be trampled on.

I shall let it go to waste, unpruned,
undug, overgrown by brambles and

thorn-bushes, and I shall command
the clouds to rain no rain on it.

Now, the vineyard of Yahweh Sabaoth
is the House of Israel, and the people of
Judah the plant he cherished. He expected
fair judgement, but found injustice, up-
rightness, but found cries of distress.

Cooker's trembling voice remained suspended
in the air, as if to emphasize the dramatic effect
of the last verse.

"I don't understand any of it," his assistant confessed, running his hand through his short hair.
"It's all Greek to me."

"Actually, you're not far off." Cooker smiled.
"It doesn't bother me all that much that you're a
nonbeliever. But not to be moved by the power of
words, that always baffles me."

"Sorry, but for me, this kind of grand speech
reminds me of old Hollywood movies. You know,
all those togas, Charlton Heston playing the
handsome hero Ben Hur fighting on his chariot,
and a bunch of skinny slaves in jock straps. I can
see the rows of cardboard colonnades as I speak!
I love it."

"All right. I don't think I'll get anything insight-
ful out of you on this subject. Your ambivalence
depresses me."

They left the annex to go to breakfast in the dining room. The weather had become milder during the night. The frayed clouds were whitish strips that revealed patches of blue sky. Aurélie welcomed them with a pretty smile and sparkling eyes that stopped Virgile in his tracks at the door. He stared at her and stammered a shy "good morning," which was not at all like him.

"Well, what's gotten into you, my boy?" Cooker whispered as he sat down.

"You didn't tell me that the welcoming committee was so charming."

"I knew you would be impressed, but I didn't want to give everything away at once."

"She's just my type."

"I have the impression they are all more or less your type. In the meantime, Virgile, get ready, because the mission awaiting you demands concentration and quite a lot of precision. I am really counting on you."

"Thank you. I take the challenge as a sign of trust."

"Most important, you are going to save me time. Please give my excuses to Olivier Lefflaive. He's a friend. He'll understand. Tell him that I have too much work to do in Vougeot and that I'll come by to say hello another time."

"I know his reputation, and he seems to be a real character, your friend Lefflaive!"

"Yes, we resemble one another somewhat. Very unusual career paths, in any case hardly typical of what people expected of us. Olivier was active in the theater circles in Paris for a long time. He's the son of a winemaking family, but he wanted to see the world, play some guitar, write songs, experience other things. Finally, the call of Burgundy was stronger than the glitz of the capital. When he returned to Puligny-Montrachet in 1984, he threw himself into his terroir like a madman and accomplished an impressive amount of work."

"It seems that his white wines are to die for."

"The reds are not bad, either. The vineyard is a very demanding business, and it's expanding. But Lefflaive and his people are down to earth, and they respect tradition. They also have a lovely motto: 'Wine teaches us respect, and the vineyard teaches us modesty.' But I won't say anymore about it. I'd rather let you discover it for yourself."

After gobbling up every morsel of their buttered bread, cleaning out a ramekin of apricot jam, and emptying their cups of tea, they left through the back door. As they passed the counter, Virgile could not resist a conspiratorial and promising wink, making the waitress blush. Cooker shrugged as he watched his assistant. Then he handed him the keys to his Mercedes and gave him some superfluous advice on how to proceed during the tasting. He waited until his purring convertible disappeared at the other end of town before heading for the Rendez-vous des Touristes Café.

When he walked in, the welcome was notably more polite than it was on his first visit. He found the same dice players sitting in front of their green felt cloth at the far corner of the bar. He took a table near the woman with the triple chin and her unassuming husband. Cooker had the feeling that he was at a re-enactment of the scene he had witnessed forty-eight hours earlier, except today they were greeting him amiably. He was now part of the landscape. Everyone knew who he was or thought they did. The night the Bravart boys were murdered, he had been seen coming out of the hotel in a bathrobe, patterned cashmere pajamas, and leather slippers. Cooker was no longer a stranger. He concluded that just having witnessed the face of death with these people was enough to create a rapport.

Cooker ordered coffee and began to chat about the weather, but the conversation soon turned to the events of the last few days. Each person gave his opinion and wanted to share it with everyone else.

"You have the right to defend yourself, but it's despicable to shoot kids!" yelled one of the dice throwers.

"He'd better be careful, that idiot Ernest," the man next to him said icily. "If I were a Bravart,

I'd make no bones about planting one between his eyes!"

"Justice will run its course," Cooker objected.

"What justice? Do you still believe in justice? It looks like he's going to get out tomorrow."

"I don't think so. He will probably be released on a bond or perhaps his own recognizance," the winemaker said. "That doesn't mean he will avoid a trial."

"He'll be watched!" the woman interjected. "And we'd better watch out, or else he'll gun down all the kids as soon as he's plastered."

"Frankly, sir, you don't kill two kids over a trifle," her husband dared to say.

"When I was young, I did worse things than write on a wall," the café owner added.

The exchange, which was growing more heated, was interrupted when a man in green overalls pushed the door open with his shoulder and barged in.

"There's firemen at Mother Grangreon's place!"

"Is it on fire?" the café owner asked, surprised.

"On ice, actually, yes!" shouted the man in overalls. "The old woman woke up under a layer of snow."

"Stop kidding, Mimile!"

"I'm serious. She was in her bed, and when she opened her eyes, she was under a layer of snow."

"What snow? It's all melted since yesterday."

"Up north, where her house is, there were still patches of snow on the slopes, and there was some near the hen house. In any case, someone dumped it on her bed. Apparently she screamed like a pig and began running all around the house. And get this, guys—all the dishes were in pieces on the floor. The furniture was turned upside down, and the curtains were pulled down. Wait till you hear the next bit: there was writing in black paint on the walls. She fainted or, I don't know, had a heart attack or something like that!"

"Writing in Latin?" Cooker asked cautiously.

"What do I know? In Latin or Chinese, who cares?"

"Is she dead?" a guy at the counter asked.

"No, but she's drooling a bit, her eyes are rolled back, and she's all stiff. It's not a pretty sight."

"Mother Grangeon never was a pretty sight," joked one of the customers.

"Let's not kid around," the café owner interrupted. "Nobody could stand Mrs. Grangeon, but we've never seen anything like this in Vougeot. Believe me, it's not a good sign!"

§ § §

Cooker spent most of his day in the village, at the Bertagna wine estate, to establish a winemaking protocol on an experimental parcel of land. He had been in touch with the managers of the property for several months and had promised to spend some time with them when he came to the area for his induction. The project was exciting and still needed some adjustments, but the cellar master and the master grower were efficient and cooperative. After long consultation and a methodical test of the decanted samples, Cooker concluded that he would definitely have to come back to Vougeot to put a final touch on this limited vintage. Before leaving, he took advantage of the opportunity to taste several vintages of Clos de la Perrière Monopole, a true Vougeot wine, which was produced outside the château but whose balance he had always appreciated.

Once back at the hotel at the end of the afternoon, he allowed himself a break in the dining room for a cup of tea. Aurélie prepared a smoky lapsang souchong, which he drank in little sips while waiting for Virgile to return. The girl made some overtures to engage him in conversation. He went along, but wasn't fooled. She finally gave herself away by casually asking one too many questions about his assistant, whose brown eyes had met hers that very morning. Cooker didn't hesitate to give her the information that she was trying hard to get out of him.

"In fact, here he is!" Cooker exclaimed as he heard the familiar sound of the convertible.

Virgile walked in with the ease of a handsome guy used to making a theatrical entrance. His gaze came to rest on Aurélie's smooth face.

"So?" Cooker said.

"Nothing but good news, sir," Virgile said, his speech mildly slurred.

"But you look smashed, my boy," Cooker said, worried.

"To be honest, I didn't leave very clearheaded. It was so fine that toward the end, I didn't have the willpower to spit. But don't worry. I didn't get behind the wheel right away. I took a little nap in the car, and the cold air woke me up."

"That's not very responsible," Cooker grumbled. "I expected more professional behavior from you! Let's see what your notes look like."

Virgile took out a bundle of pages that his boss almost tore from his hands.

"Very cool atmosphere. I got along very well with Pascal Wagner. He's a super sommelier. We talked about rock 'n' roll almost as much as we talked about wine."

The assistant was effusive and joyfully related his visit with Olivier Lefflaive. The wine tasting had taken place before a nice plate of local cured meats, Bresse chicken stewed in honey, and several local cheeses.

Cooker was not really listening to him and consulted the sheets to see if they were in order.

"Well, I am going to my room to read all of this in peace. Tonight I am skipping dinner. I decided to diet today, and considering your state, I suggest you do the same."

Once in his room, Cooker raised the thermostat, took off his shoes, pulled on a cashmere sweater, and stretched out on his bed to study his employee's report. Everything was recorded according to Cooker & Co. criteria. He began with the tasting of the whites, which had been lined up in the 1999 vintage: Meursault, Chassagne-Montrachet, Puligny-Montrachet, Chassagne premier cru Blanchots, Meursault premier cru Charmes, and Puligny-Montrachet premier cru Chalumeaux. The notes were well written, both technical and perceptive, and some made the winemaker smile.

Virgile's notes were as pertinent as they were impertinent. Chablis grand cru Valmur 2000: "Rather citrusy, mineral, with a touch of sweetness, a bit creamy. Superb bouquet. (You could say fabulous without exaggerating too much.) Floral, round, balanced. Very satisfying structure." In the margin he had scribbled a note that was crossed out. Cooker could still make it out: "Think of asking Mom what perfume she wore when I was in high school. Same lemony, slightly acidic, smooth smell."

Cooker could see that the finale of the wine-tasting session had been a real joy: Puligny-Montrachet premier cru Pucelles, Corton-Charlemagne grand cru, and Bienvenues-Bâtard-Montrachet grand cru in four successive vintages. Sublime whites that brought the art of chardonnay winemaking to unexpected heights. They were sometimes difficult to spit out. Virgile had done good work. Admittedly, his conduct had been a bit less than stellar, or at least he had drunk without much moderation. But he had written an impeccable wine-tasting report that was sufficiently precise and analytical without losing his personality and refined subjectivity. Obviously, this young man from Bergerac felt comfortable in Burgundy. He understood its authenticity, its rough manners, its gruff simplicity, and its down-to-earth honesty that emphasized doing what you say, not saying what you do.

Cooker placed the notes on his bedside table, picked up his cell phone, and punched in the number for Robert Bressel, the reporter. Night would soon fall on Vougeot.

"Good evening, Mr. Bressel."

"Ah, Mr. Cooker!"

"How did you know it was me?"

"I have an ear for voices. I only have to hear one once to recognize it among thousands."

In the background, there was the muffled sound of a sitar mixed with the banging of a tabla.

Cooker had no trouble imagining the heady odor of patchouli. He rubbed his nose in irritation.

"I heard about what happened last night at Mrs. Grangeon's place," Cooker said. "How is the good woman doing?"

"Good woman? Who says?"

"I don't know her, to tell you the truth. But what happened to her is still very strange."

"That old lady has a reputation as a battle-ax and nasty shrew. Mean to everyone, including family. But no one wishes her any harm. At the moment, she is still at the hospital in a state of shock. I just finished my article, and I had to hold off a bit, because the doctors don't want to comment just yet. We only know that her heart is not about to give out."

"That's good."

"Apparently, the less heart you have, the stronger it is."

"I have the impression that this latest episode completely exonerates the two boys. In my opinion, they died for nothing—just for having been smart alecks."

"That's my opinion, too, but it seems to me that the police are still on that track. I inquired myself, and it appears that Cedric was more or less a dunce, but his cousin, David, was an excellent student: baccalaureate with honors, seven years of Latin, and good grades throughout, right on schedule for catechism, first communion, and confirmation. In short, a completely plausible suspect. And besides, his name was David."

"Maybe," Cooker conceded. "But it doesn't necessarily follow that he would know all those psalms. Still, what a waste. Those poor kids!"

"Getting back to Adèle Grangeon, I think the staging is a bit crude."

"What are you insinuating?"

"As if someone meant to add a layer of complications, offer a whole new set of clues, and send yet another message to decode."

"What are you getting at?"

"Nothing, but I have the feeling that there is something to pursue here. The graffiti messages that they found at Grangeon's place correspond to the missing second and third verses from Psalm 102. I tried to reach my nephew to get some information. I already told you about him. He's the one who works at the regional library. He did his thesis on the folklore of Burgundy and the secret histories of the Côte-d'Or. I'm sure he's got something to say about this."

"What's his name again?"

"Pierre-Jean Bressel. You can find him during the day in the offices of the historical collections."

"Excuse me for belaboring the point, but there is still something strange about Mrs. Grangeon. How is it that she didn't wake up in the night?"

"It seems that she's been taking sleeping pills since her husband died. She must have been sleeping like a rock."

"I see."

The two men sketched out some more theories without much basis, then decided they had examined the case from all angles. Soon after hanging up, Cooker called his wife to confirm that he would, indeed, return home the following weekend. He missed Elisabeth, and he told her so tenderly and discreetly. Then he asked about his dog, Bacchus, and whether the first buds were blooming along the paths of their home, Grangebelle. Cooker knew that Elisabeth would pick up the melancholy in his voice and want to know how this trip to Burgundy was unfolding. He responded vaguely. She pressed him a bit. Benjamin reassured her, "Everything is going well, my sweet. Nothing to report."

7

The dining room was deserted, the shutters closed, the tables empty, and the coffeemaker turned off. Cooker waited for a few minutes and decided to go back and awaken Virgile. When he turned into the passageway that led to the courtyard, he spotted the furtive silhouette of Aurélie hurrying nervously from the annex. She smoothed her hair before slipping through the back door.

Cooker sighed and walked directly to his assistant's room. He knocked several times without getting a response. He turned the doorknob and found that the door wasn't locked. Cooker poked his head in and surveyed the scene. The bed had slid toward the chest of drawers. The rumpled sheets were spilling onto the floor, and the pillows had been tossed to the other side of the room. The sound of a vigorous shower was coming from the bathroom, joyously accompanied by off-key whistling. Virgile was merrily butchering the melody from *The Bridge Over the River Kwaï.*

"That's right, my boy, the sun is shining, shining, shining," Cooker sang softly as he closed the door.

When he returned to the dining room, Aurélie was bustling behind the counter and putting the breakfast rolls in wicker baskets.

"Sorry, sir, I was late. Your tea will be ready in a few minutes."

"No rush," he said and watched, amused, as she laid out the tray with feverish movements that were so unlike her. "I hope it was nothing serious?"

"No, sir, just couldn't find my watch."

"Ah, Aurélie, time flies when we're having fun!" he teased.

The young woman paid no attention and approached the table with an angelic smile. Her pink face, luminous blue eyes, pulled-back hair, and round mouth gave her the honest but still mysterious look of a polychromatic virgin in a Romanesque church.

Virgile appeared in a heady cloud of Italian cologne. He waved to his boss enthusiastically. He gave the waitress a sidelong greeting that was both subtle and awkward as he walked past the counter. Aurélie blushed and lowered her head to dry a stack of saucers. Virgile focused on devouring his pastries. He drank two glasses of orange juice and served himself cup after cup of tea.

"One would think you haven't eaten in a week," Cooker said. "Build up your strength. You seem to need it."

"Did you read my notes?"

"Yes, and I congratulate you. It's quite unexpected, considering your condition last night. I hope you got your beauty sleep?"

Virgile ignored the question and asked about the plan for the day.

"We are going to Dijon!" Cooker announced as he was getting up. "And we shouldn't sit around too long."

The engine of the Mercedes was already running when the young man trotted out of the hotel, a croissant in his mouth and his jacket half on.

"You think of nothing but eating, my boy!" Cooker said. "Come on. We're off!"

Comfortably stretched out in the convertible's burnished-leather seat, the assistant pulled a stack of raisin cakes out of his pocket.

"That young girl spoils you, Virgile. Please don't take advantage of her generosity."

They arrived without mishap in the historic center of Dijon and had no trouble finding a place to park. The winemaker gave some free time to his assistant, who felt duty-bound to visit the former Palace of the Dukes of Burgundy and its fine arts museum. Cooker intended to see the reporter's nephew at the regional library, which was not far away.

Once he got there, a receptionist showed him to the office where Pierre-Jean Bressel presided. At the back, to the right of shelves dedicated to the history of Burgundy, a gray silhouette was seated at a table. Cooker approached slowly to get a good look at the archivist, who was filing piles of documents. The man was no more than thirty. He had a moon-shaped face, slightly flabby jowls, and thick bifocal glasses that distorted his face. His greasy hair was plastered to his skull. Robert Bressel's nephew seemed to belong to another era. As he rose slowly, Bressel's shoulders remained stooped, as if the centuries were weighing them down.

"Hello, sir. May I help you?" His monotone voice exhaled dust and melancholy.

"Hello, young man. I was sent here by your Uncle Robert. He interviewed me in Vougeot a few days ago, and he recommended that I meet you in order to—"

"I know," Pierre-Jean Bressel interrupted. "You are Mr. Cooker, aren't you? He called me, and I have been expecting you, more or less."

"I was in the area for a meeting in Dijon," Cooker lied with impressive composure. "I hope I am not disturbing you."

"Not in the least. I suppose that you want to talk about the events that have taken place recently."

"Absolutely. It seems that you have worked for a long time on the folklore of Burgundy and that you might be able to shed some light on certain matters for us."

"I do not know if I am able to help you, but I have, in fact, studied certain phenomena that come from legends or beliefs. Let's say mysteries, if anything."

"Do you think that what happened to Adèle Grangeon might be in your area of expertise?"

"I am just a historian and do not claim to be anything more, but it does seem to correspond with other events that took place long ago. It's not the first time that snow has been found on a bed in a home where the furniture has also been moved, and dishes have been broken. There have been many instances of this sort, most notably one that happened in 1826 in the town of Pluvet. Many houses were found this way, with snow on beds and other furniture. The residents said the devil had visited them. Some even claimed to have been hit by rocks in their sleep."

"And what did that mean?"

"We do not know any more about it."

The librarian pushed up his thick glasses, which had slipped down his nose. He smoothed his oily hair and extracted a file from a stack.

"This dissertation deals with several other matters of this sort," he said in a toneless voice that was beginning to irritate Cooker. "I will spare you the chapter on the haunted houses. There are so many of them. But one particular story might be noteworthy. Back in 1633, a Chrétien Bochot, who ran an inn on the Rue de la Bretonnerie in Beaune, was complaining of nightly disturbances. Each morning, he would find trunks and furniture turned upside down and dishes thrown on the floor. Luckily, in those days, dishes were made of pewter, so they didn't break. But the noise must have been terrifying. He also said he heard things: whimpering, chains rattling, groans, and screams from the attic."

"So, what happened?"

"After that, we don't know."

"In the end, no one knows anything," Cooker said, both disappointed and annoyed.

"We suspect some things."

"But you don't have a vaguely rational explanation?"

"By cross-referencing, we have observed that there is always a child connected to the story, sometimes several."

"Could the children have been playing dirty tricks to frighten people? A little like the two young Bravart kids in some way?"

"Not at all. It was just observed that children were in the vicinity. There are three more recent examples. In 1877 in Chauvirey, a man who took in a little girl from a social-service agency was the target of the same type of harassment. He heard scratching, footsteps, and a terrifying racket every night for several months. They called in a soothsayer, a sort of exorcist, who concluded that the noise manifested only when the child was in bed and that it was her spirit acting up."

"And there, same thing," Cooker interrupted wearily. "You're going to tell me that we know nothing more about it."

Pierre-Jean Bressel did not respond but rather readjusted his glasses and turned some pages of the dissertation.

"We also know that in 1898 in La Roche-en-Brenil, a Mr. Garrie, who was a weaver by trade, saw his clock shake and fall to the floor and his lamps suddenly go out. He relit the lamps and put the clock back up. But the same thing happened. He called his neighbors over, and they watched as the furnishings tumbled over, and pictures came off the walls. Then a hammer sprang out of a drawer, broke a window, and ended up in the street."

"That's disturbing," the winemaker admitted, leaning over the document.

"I have some press clippings from the time of the incident. See for yourself. The events occurred over the span of several days: tables knocked over, jars of pickles smashed, sideboard upside down."

"Was there a child involved that time?"

"Yes, a youngster from the hospice who was raised by the family. As soon as he was sent to Saulieu, there were no more incidents. There were also several children in the home of Mr.

Girard in Aubigny-la-Ronce. On the night of every Sabbath there were terrifying noises that everyone heard. One of them was a sound like collapsing logs, as if someone were knocking over entire stacks of firewood. It always happened as soon as Mr. Girard's daughter-in-law put the grandchildren to bed."

"And yet there was no writing on the walls, as there was in Vougeot," Cooker remarked, trying to look Pierre-Jean in the eye behind the Coke-bottle glasses.

"Indeed, that may be a new element that should be indexed."

"So there is no historical incident, proven or imagined, that involves the Psalms of David?"

"As far as I know, not one. We find many legends that revolve around the devil, satyrs, suspicious ceremonies and nights of debauchery. There are also quite a few tales of ghosts, such as a certain lady in white who wanders the countryside. From time to time, she is dressed in black instead of white. But is this really the same phantom? There is no dearth of shocking occurrences and bizarre apparitions—stories of tortured saints, trials, and stakes, talking crucifixes, fake Virgin Marys, bodies risen from the dead, what have you. Herders of wolves, goblins, spirits, and miraculous springs."

"You are talking about superstitions and rumors, whereas what we have here are not hoaxes. Your stories don't appear to be relevant."

"You should consult Lucien Filongey. He's a man who claims to be an expert in the field, and he easily invokes celestial forces. He deals with all those things that worry the common mortal."

"Where can I find him?"

"Ask anyone in Gilly-lès-Cîteaux. They'll tell you how to get to his place."

"Filongey, you say?"

"Yes, Lucien Filongey: part bonesetter, part magician, part exorcist. You won't find a more interesting man!"

"This part of the country never ceases to surprise me," Cooker said, nodding. "I was familiar, or so I thought, with its wine spirit, but I didn't know about the…divine spirits."

"That's amusing," Pierre-Jean conceded soberly. "The novelist Stendhal, who knew this region extremely well, was not very fond of our countryside. But he was a great admirer of the wines of Clos de Vougeot. Incidentally, he wrote something very true: 'As I left Dijon I stared hard at the famous Côte-d'Or, so celebrated throughout Europe. I had to recall the verse, "Are witty people ever ugly?" for without its wonderful wines, I would find nothing uglier than the Côte d'Or.'"

"You have an excellent memory," Cooker said with admiration. "Perhaps that is why you immediately recognized Psalm 102?"

"Stendhal also wrote this: 'At the table, Burgundians speak only about wines, their comparative merits, their faults, and their qualities; boring politics, so impolite in the provinces, are left aside.'"

"I thank you for all of your valuable information, Mr. Bressel, but I must go."

"It was a pleasure," murmured the librarian.

As soon as he had left the building, Cooker took a deep breath of fresh air. His feet planted solidly on the sidewalk, he stood for a long moment, turning over in his mind this conversation, which had seemed far too rambling. He started walking without paying attention to the passersby or the half-timbered homes and shops of the old city, which would have fascinated him on any other occasion. His phone rang at the bottom of his coat pocket.

"Are you finished with your meeting, sir?"

"Where are you, Virgile?"

"I'm buying mustard."

"You are?"

"Well, yes. In Dijon, it seems appropriate. I'm getting a jar of it for my sister, Raphaëlle. She loves it. I am at the Maille shop."

Cooker walked up the Rue de la Liberté and spotted Virgile behind the magnificent store

window that had flaunted its letters of gastronomic nobility since the nineteenth century. The
fluttering salesgirls seemed to be greatly enjoying
themselves in the company of this handsome
young man with an imposing build but reassuring
long eyelashes. He was bewitching them with his
distinctively southwestern French accent. Virgile
emerged, beaming.

"I also got a jar for Mrs. Cooker. She likes it,
I hope."

"Even if she hated mustard, she would pretend
to appreciate it, because you're the one giving it
to her. Be careful, or I'll start getting jealous."

"Come on, Mr. Cooker. She could be my mother." Virgile burst out laughing.

"With you, you can never know, Virgile. No
woman can resist you. Or is it the other way
around?"

"You exaggerate, sir. But honestly, those wom-
en were charming," he added with a wink.

"So, what did you think of the Dukes of
Burgundy Palace?"

"Not much. I decided to stroll down the streets
instead."

"And no museums, either?"

"Sorry to disappoint you, but without you, it's
not as much fun."

"Never mind. You're not going to get out of it
that easily. We're going there right away!"

"But I had no intention of avoiding it, boss."

They quickly ate panini sandwiches with goat cheese and dashed off to the Ducal Palace. Cooker did not want his young assistant to miss any of the galleries. Without overwhelming Virgile too much with commentary, Cooker gave him an overall idea of what he needed to know so as not to die an idiot. Cooker spent some time examining the *Presentation of the Infant Jesus in the Temple*, painted by Philippe de Champaigne, while Virgile lingered even longer before an anonymous painting from the Renaissance, simply titled *Woman at Her Toilet*. They both came out of the palace inspired but exhausted.

Virgile said that nothing was better for re-energizing than a good walk, preferably at a brisk pace. Cooker went along with the idea and even decided to walk double time through the churches of Notre-Dame and Saint-Philibert and the Saint Benignus Cathedral. They found their car not far from Place Bossuet, close to the neighborhood that used to be frequented by "blue bottoms," as wine growers used to be called in Dijon. It formerly housed the wine growers trade organization.

Night had fallen without warning, and the streetlights were already lit. Cooker suggested taking a detour to the Castel de Très Girard, which Virgile could not very well refuse. On the way, they chatted like satisfied tourists, and then Cooker told Virgile about his meeting at the library. He shared his reservations about the librarian with the chubby face, shiny hair, and thick binocular glasses.

"I have a bad feeling. I almost have the impression that he was saying a lot but not revealing anything. Maybe I wasn't listening the way I should have been, or perhaps I wasn't picking up what he was saying between the lines. He was a strange guy: polite and friendly, yes, but evasive, elusive even."

"You must have been frustrated," Virgile concluded.

"Not really. It was more that I had the impression that he wanted to lead the discussion in a certain direction and not really talk about the reason I had come to see him."

When they arrived in Morey-Saint-Denis, they parked in front of the Castel de Très Girard and finished their conversation before going into the restaurant. Cooker asked about Raphaëlle, Virgil's sister. He knew that she had a serious medical condition, and he had lit a candle for her in the chapel of the cathedral that very afternoon.

"Thank you, sir. She is doing better, and we're hopeful. Between your candle and my jar of mustard, she has been spoiled today!"

The owner greeted them with open arms. "Sorry that I wasn't here to greet you the other day. It was my night off. How are you, Benjamin? It's been more than a year."

Although he had not been born in Burgundy, Sébastien Pilat was an expert in the habits and customs of the land he had adopted. An impressive understanding of wine and a decided taste for well-crafted cigars complemented his gastronomic knowledge. It was obvious that he had taken over the reins of this establishment with the goal of making it one of the best in Côte-de-Nuits. And his hard work, innovation, and high standards were paying off.

"The other night we ate entirely too much here at your restaurant," Cooker said as he unfolded his napkin on his lap. "We've come back to do penance!"

Cooker ordered just one course and a dessert, but Virgile opted for the entire regional meal. A marc de Bourgogne granita allowed him to recharge his appetite halfway through. When it was time for coffee, Sébastien Pilat invited them into the private back room, where he offered them their choice of cigars from his humidor. The winemaker chose a Cohiba Esplendido and suggested that his assistant take a Flor de Copan Linea Puros. The distinguished Honduran cigar was a final intermediate step before the Havanas of the big island. Settled in their club chairs, which were facing the fireplace, the three men watched the flames dancing while they talked pleasantly about the renovations that Sébastien was planning, which would improve this little eighteenth-century mansion even more. Then they got around to the gossip that was swirling in the villages of the Côte. Cooker admitted that he was very interested in all these stories, and in the course of the discussion, Sébastien asked them innocently, "Did you hear that Honoré Mancenot, Ernest's brother, was found dead tonight?"

Cooker and Virgile looked at him, incredulous. They simultaneously let out a big cloud of white smoke, their cigars frozen between their fingers.

"It was dark out, and a driver spotted his moped lying on its side on the shoulder of the road. The old man was in the ditch, his head smashed against a big rock. A phrase in Latin was painted on the pavement."

"What phrase?" asked Cooker, sounding worried.

"Honestly, I wouldn't know, but it was definitely in Latin. A retired professor from Morey confirmed it."

"Someone talked to me today about a man named Lucien Filongey," Cooker said, taking great care not to let the ashes from his Churchill fall on his shirt. "Do you know him?"

"Who doesn't know him? It's said that he heals burns and resets fractures. There might be some truth to it, or else he wouldn't have so many clients. Some people also say that he performs rituals that are, well, let's just say not very orthodox."

"I'd like to meet him, but I'm not sure how to go about it."

Putting his finger on his lips and frowning as if to concentrate better, Sébastien thought for a moment. "If you don't want to arouse suspicion, there is a simple solution. Just take a bottle of wine to him to release from a spell."

"Are you serious?"

"The old people around here still resort to this practice from time to time. It's rare now, but it was common years ago in the countryside. Filongey knows all the prayers for chasing away evil spirits. He's a strange guy. You'll see. If you want to contact him without looking like a busybody, all you need to do is remove the label from any bottle. Take it to him, and have him do his prayer. Make it up as you go, and get him to talk!"

"You mean to say that I have to get a bottle of wine exorcised to worm something out of this charlatan?"

"If you really want to mine the depths of darkness, I don't see any other solution."

"It keeps getting better," Cooker said and sighed as he threw what remained of his cigar into the flames.

8

The man was wiry and tall, slightly stooped but chin up. His lean torso was squeezed into a black satin shirt. Pearl buttons shimmered under the glare of the candelabras.

His weather-beaten face, with its angular cheekbones and prominent nose, was not animated by any particular expression. It wasn't clear whether he was friendly or aloof; he seemed beyond ordinary appraisal, just simply indifferent, absent from the world.

"Welcome to the house of divine help, gentlemen."

Cooker and Virgile walked into a large room with dark velvet curtains that seemed to be breathing in the flickering glow of the candelabras. Before a wooden screen, a grinning skull and open prayer book lay upon a desk. A string of ebony rosary beads was draped around an image of the Virgin of Lourdes. Above her, a boxwood wreath was drying.

"You must be the gentlemen from Bordeaux," Lucien Filongey said curtly.

Virgile shuddered, but Cooker refused to let himself be spooked. He figured the sorcerer of Gilly read *Le Bien Public* newspaper, just as everyone else did. One did not have to be a seer to know who the two men were.

"Yes, you are aware that we are on a business trip in this region, but we find ourselves in a bit of a fix."

The man crossed his arms and stared at them.

"We've tried everything," Cooker continued, trying to sound distressed. "But this particular wine concerns me—I brought you a sample. It's evolving in a way we just don't understand. I was told you could help, and maybe rid the wine of whatever evil has possessed it."

"Your science has its limits." Filongey sneered.

"I agree," Cooker replied humbly.

"Place your bottle on the table, and stand back."

The shaman seized a vial of water, sprayed his hands, and held them around the bottle without touching it. He remained this way for more than ten minutes, in absolute silence, before declaring in a rumbling voice, "Our help comes from the Lord, who made Heaven and earth. I exorcise you, living wine, through the One who, at the wedding at Cana in Galilee, changed the water into excellent wine, through Him to whom the Jews gave wine mixed with gall, so that no secrets may be exchanged with the evil spirits, so that you may be wine that is healthful and cure all God's creatures who may drink of it. Dismiss, oh Lord, every evil spell, incantation, impotence, fracture, ague, infection, distress, curse, satanic act, convulsion, and all other infirmities of the body and soul. Through Jesus Christ our Lord. Amen."

He had delivered his entire speech in one breath. His eyes were wide open, trained on the neck of the bottle.

"Hear us, Lord, and grant your benevolence to those who ask for it, and look favorably on your creature tormented by the devil, and spread on this wine your blessings and your sanctification. I bless this wine and sanctify it in your name so that the demons will be expelled and their evil spells will be broken."

Virgile pursed his lips to stifle the laugh that was rising in his throat. He would not be able to contain it much longer. Cooker gave him a swift kick on the shin with his Lobbs. The young man paled. Filongey continued.

"You have planted the vine and have surrounded it with care from the beginning, and in times of drought, you have watered it with the divine blood of Your Son. Deign then, Lord, to bless this fruit of the grape so that it may be the wine of mercy, science, doctrine, devotion, love, and virtue to cure all creatures who will drink of it, so that it will nourish the soul and fortify faith, that it will sustain the body, that it will enlighten the mind, make the heart rejoice, chase away pain and sorrow, and destroy all evil in those creatures who will drink of it. Through You, the all powerful and everlasting God. So be it."

"Amen," Virgile let out. He could not stand it any longer and was ready to say anything to get rid of his nervous tension.

"Thank you very much, Mr. Filongey," said Cooker, who had managed to keep his British stiff upper lip. "I have no doubt that your prayer will be invaluable to us."

"I will pray for you tomorrow at the same hour. Our good country of Burgundy must be saved from the workings of the devil."

"It's true that Vougeot has not been spared, lately."

"The good Adèle Grangeon received a visit from him two nights ago. Beware—the devil may be lurking among the vineyards!"

"We will be vigilant," Cooker promised. "I would not want to suffer the same fate as that poor woman or the old man they found dead in a ditch last night."

"The Prince of Darkness strikes the pure and the impure alike. I prayed for the salvation of the soul of our good Adèle, who did not deserve such a fate. A pious woman who never forgets to go to Mass and say her prayers to the Black Virgin."

"The Bravart cousins were also devout Christians," the winemaker ventured.

Lucien Filongey turned red and waved his arms. His tunic came undone, giving him the look of a nighthawk poised to swoop down on its prey. He bellowed, "Children of cursed childbirth! Not one of them legitimate! Bastards! Detritus of whores! The Mancenot brothers are nothing but sodomites, traitors! Bigots!"

He stopped suddenly and stared at one of the candelabras as if the mere power of his lunatic gaze could extinguish the flames. Then, in a softened voice, he said, "Shh! Gentlemen, Satan is listening to us." His tone turned unctuous, making him sound all the more disturbing. "The Evil One is among us. He lurks and observes us, just waiting to find a home in malevolent spirits."

"We thank you again for your intercession, Mr. Filongey."

"The world of wine is quite wrong to deprive itself of my services. The winemakers do not know what they are missing. In the past—I'm talking about ancient times—there wasn't a single wine in this land that did not have recourse to divine protection. Do you know that it was the priests of the diocese who would save the vineyard by putting a curse on the flies, the weevils, and the *escrivains*?"

"The *escrivains*, you say?" interrupted the winemaker, who could never resist the chance to enrich his cultural knowledge, no matter where he was or the circumstances.

"Yes, it's a name they used for little evil brown and black beetles. They called them scribblers because they left little markings on the vine leaves. The Clos de Vougeot suffered much and it was a great misfortune, gentlemen! Whenever the vines were withering under the vermin, and the leaves were devoured, people would have processions. They would forbid using the name of the Lord in vain and everyone went to confession. Purifying, cleansing, and sanctifying the soul—this is what we need to bring back today."

It was time to leave, Cooker thought as he reached for his bottle. Filongey gave them an icy smile.

"Before you leave, gentlemen, I would like to offer you two excellent wine tonics that I made myself. I macerate a good quarter gallon of red arrière-côte for about ten days with about two and a half ounces of fennel seeds. And for the white, I always use one from the slopes of Beaune. I add slices of fresh kola nut with a little *eau-de-vie*. Tell me how you like it, since you are the experts."

"We won't forget," Cooker said and nodded, eager to leave.

"Every person I have given it to has benefited from it. Believe me, it's the only remedy for severe exhaustion and anemia. It's better than other tonics, even cod liver oil and horse blood. All those potions rot in the stomach and cause pestilential gas, inflammation of the uterus in women, vaginal discharge in young girls, and extreme diarrhea in young boys. I can assure you that my fortifying wines are safe! You only need to take one shot glass of it twice a day, preferably at ten in the morning and four in the afternoon."

"Many thanks, Mr. Filongey," Cooker said, faking a grin.

"May the All Mighty protect you, and don't forget to drink at least one glass of magnetized water every day."

Virgile let out an immense sigh of relief as soon as he closed the car door.

"That nutcase freaked me out!"

"I confess, he didn't put my mind at ease, either," Cooker said as he stomped on the gas.

Virgile put the two vials of Lucien Filongey's tonic in the backseat and turned to his boss, letting out a nervous laugh.

"Holy shit. I bet these two bottles will get rated nineteen out of twenty in the next *Cooker Guide*!"

9

The rounds of wine tasting in the Morey-Saint-Denis vineyards appellation would begin later than planned. Lucien Filongey's ranting was still troubling the two men from Bordeaux, and they were struggling to concentrate on the work they had to do. Before they reached the Clos de la Bidaude, they slowed down to look for the place where Honoré Mancenot had met his death. Halfway between Vougeot and Morey, they saw the writing in black paint that ran across the pavement. They stopped short on the embankment.

In his notebook Benjamin Cooker wrote down the Latin phrase that stretched in three segments across the gravel carpet.

Deus virtutum convertere:
respice de caelo, et vide,
et visita veneam istam
Et perfice eam, quam plantavit dextera tua: et
super filium hominis, quem confirmasti tibi

*Incensa igni et suffossa ab increpatione vultus
tui peribunt.*

"What are you thinking about, boss?"

"It must have taken a lot of time to write such a long passage."

"You can't say there's heavy traffic on this road. You could write a book in between the time two cars go by!"

"Maybe. In any case, the person who wrote this has an impressive memory and serious knowledge. There's no doubt about that."

"And you're forgetting something," Virgile said. "He believes in God."

"In God or the devil," grumbled Cooker.

"At any rate, as for the phenomenal memory, I agree with you. I don't see the guy holding his Bible in his left hand and writing with a spray can in his right. And also, it couldn't have been easy in the middle of the night, in the dark."

"Maybe he used his headlights to help him?"

"I don't know. It looks to me like he was just trying to get it down," Virgile said. "The way you just want to get something down when you observe a wine and take your notes without looking at your notebook. You see, in this spot, the writing is more spread out, as if he had to go faster. Maybe he heard a car coming. There, he hurried. Everything was written in one shot. The letters are strung together. Here, again, it's very clear. And there, false alarm: the sound of the engine must have grown more distant, and he ended less frantically. The letters are more rounded in the last words. There is even a period."

"After such an explanation, my boy, what can I add?"

Cooker checked to see if he had correctly transcribed the text and walked over to the embankment. The grass was still flat in some places. Perhaps old Mancenot's moped had slid the length of it. He had probably gone down near the distance marker. He could make out a faint sign of impact. The body had surely rolled all the way down to the pile of rocks, where there were still large traces of blood. Cooker went back to the Mercedes, where his assistant was already searching for a radio station that would spare him the umpteenth tear-jerking scene from *La Traviata*.

"I don't want to tell you what to do, but we're going to be late, sir."

"You are right, Virgile. Our work awaits us. But I forgot something in my room."

They stopped briefly at the Hotel de Vougeot. Cooker jumped out without turning the engine off and reappeared quickly with his Bible. He put the car in first, ground the gears, and headed off toward the secondary road.

The plan for the day was entirely dedicated to the terroir of Morey-Saint-Denis, and a long itinerary lay before them. Virgile had taken care to organize the visits by calling all the estates that Cooker wanted to discover or study in depth for the new edition of the guide. Their side trip to the scene of the tragedy had disrupted their schedule. Now there was no time to waste, and they had to get down to business: taste without lingering, avoid long conversations, remember to get the informational brochures for all the wineries, file the notes immediately, and, if possible, get additional samples to back up their opinions once they returned to Bordeaux.

They went from one tasting to the next with almost military rigor. Virgile spat without a single lapse of protocol. More than once, however, he did wax enthusiastic about some cru that deserved to be more closely examined.

Having read his boss's works attentively, he knew perfectly well that the village of Morey-Saint-Denis constituted one of the smallest communal appellations of the Côte-de-Nuits. At the Vinexpo exhibition and during advanced training courses given by the faculty of oenology, he had been able to taste the five particular appellations that were part of the terroir: Clos de Tart, Clos Saint-Denis, Bonnes-Mares, Clos de la Roche, and Clos des Lambrays. These five red wines alone, classified as grands crus, brought together the qualities of the two prestigious appellations on either side of them. The nature of the terrain could be tasted in the wine. They had the

intensity and the power of a Gevrey-Chambertin
without losing the finesse and elegance of a
Chambolle-Musigny.

Virgile had never before faced so much Morey-
Saint-Denis in so little time: a Clos de la Bidaude,
one of Guy Coquard's Les Blanchards, several
vintages of the Dujac estate, as well as Domaine
Alain Jeanniard, the cuvées En La Rue de Vergy
from the Lignier-Michelot winery, Aux Charmes
from Pierre Amiot et Fils, Les Millandes de
Palisses-Beaumont, and Henri Perrot-Minot's La
Riotte Vieilles Vignes. All these terroirs, which
the Burgundians called *"climats,"* contained
enough aromatic marvels and richness to satisfy
the most sophisticated palate. Virgile was there-
fore attentive and picked up several samples in order to continue exploring when he got back home.
While he was finishing his list of small bottles and
filing the cards at the Beaumont estate's wine
warehouses, Cooker retreated to the car.

Benjamin was feeling weary. In his mouth, he
could still taste a nice vintage that had had a sus-
tained color and somewhat woody flavor. It was
becoming cooked fruit, a bit like jam, with hints
of vanilla. The nose had opened on notes of cassis
and spices. Despite the sweetness on his palate, he
was preoccupied with the writing discovered on
the road. He had been thinking about it continu-
ously while he worked. He pulled out his fountain
pen and began translating, resolving as best he

could the problems of syntax. Then he reached for his Bible in the glove compartment and consulted the psalms one by one, concentrating intensely. His index finger ran down the length of the pages with a regular cadence so that he would not miss the passage. Many minutes went by before his finger stopped at Psalm Eighty, lines fourteen through sixteen.

> God Sabaoth, come back,
> we pray, look down from heaven and see,
> visit this vine;
> protect what your own hand has planted.
> They have thrown it on the fire like dung,
> the frown of your rebuke will destroy them.

He went over the text several times in its entirety and remembered having read it many years earlier. It was a prayer for the restoration of Israel, a heartfelt plea for justice. Nothing in the text where the vineyard was invoked managed to awaken in him the least hint of a clue. He got out of his car, pulled out his cell phone, and punched in the number for Robert Bressel as he strode through the courtyard across from the farmhouse. He motioned for his assistant to hurry up as he waited for Bressel to answer.

"Hello," he said simply, since Bressel claimed to have an ear for voices.

"Mr. Cooker, good timing! I just came back this minute from the police station in Nuits-Saint-Georges, and there's lots of excitement there.

"The investigation is making progress?"

"They took some photos of the graffiti and made enlargements so that the handwriting specialists could analyze them. According to my information, nothing jumped out at them."

"They couldn't say if it was the same person each time?"

"I am pretty close to the captain," Bressel explained. "But he doesn't tell me everything."

"However, that is an important point." Cooker's words remained suspended in silence. "Hello?"

"I'm still here, Mr. Cooker. I am weighing what you just said. Do you think that the latest writing on the road might not have been written by the same person?"

"It's just a theory. They don't exactly match. But maybe it's because of the way the writing was done."

"I am not following your reasoning," the reporter confessed.

"Writing on a vertical surface with a can of spray paint would have to differ slightly from writing on a horizontal surface. You understand? The act of bending over and tipping the can has to modify the handwriting. That's without even considering the conditions, which had to be challenging. There was more urgency."

"That makes sense, especially since it all happened at nightfall, around seven-thirty, according to the autopsy report. It was still early, and there was a bit of traffic."

"That's what I was thinking. I went to the scene, and if you examine everything very carefully, you notice some nuances, slight changes, compared with the graffiti in Vougeot and Gilly. Unfortunately, I haven't seen the writing at Adèle Grangeon's."

"You seem to be giving this matter a lot of thought," Bressel observed in a tone that could be interpreted as respectful, intrigued, or sarcastic.

"I can't help it," Cooker responded a bit curtly. "And by the way, I also had the chance to see your nephew in Dijon. Strange boy!"

"Pierre-Jean is a brilliant young man, but he has never had much luck. He deserves more than that job at the library, and I think he is bored there."

"He told me a lot of interesting stories, but I didn't learn anything. I had the impression that he was taking me for a ride."

"I'm surprised to hear that. That's not like him."

"What I mean is that he didn't give me any leads, and he kept changing direction. At the end of the day, I felt a bit lost."

"Pierre-Jean never says anything without a reason, so that surprises me. Perhaps he didn't have any insights."

"Possibly. Did he talk to you about our meeting?" the winemaker asked as he signaled to Virgile to put the cases in the trunk of the convertible.

"No, I haven't spoken to him since your visit."

"You don't see each other regularly?"

"Very rarely. He's pretty introverted. He lives in his books and doesn't mix with people much. He has a hard time with his looks, and I am afraid he'll end up a bachelor. It's true that he has never been attractive. He was in love once, a girl in his class, but she went off and married some wife-beater. He's good-natured, though, and remarkably sensitive. I think he never quite recovered from the blow of not getting the job of curator of the historical archives."

"That's an important position for a young historian," Cooker said.

"Indeed, and he worked very hard for it. He passed all his exams brilliantly and submitted a dissertation that received a special award from the jury. The position should have gone to him. I have always suspected some maneuvering went on."

"Who was named in his place?"

"The grandson of a prominent regional politician who's the mayor of a town near Nuits-Saint-Georges and a big wine trader. I'm sure he influenced the administrative authorities who made the decision."

"I see."

115

"That said, his grandson was not a bad student. He was a decent candidate, but he hadn't really distinguished himself on the exam. At any rate, the scores have never been made public. Just one mention in the *Journal Officiel*. But why am I telling you all this?"

The winemaker did not answer. Robert Bressel cleared his throat and excused himself on the pretext of having to meet a deadline for the next day's paper.

"I'll be sure to buy *Le Bien Public* to have the pleasure of reading your article," Cooker said by way of good-bye.

10

"This time they attacked the château, Mr. Cooker!" Aurélie shouted this without taking the time to greet him. She was trembling, and Cooker didn't know if she was frightened by the events or simply excited by so much activity in so few days.

"What happened?" the winemaker asked.

"There are firemen, and policemen, and other cars, and—"

"Are all those people up there? At the Château du Clos de Vougeot?"

"Yes, Mr. Cooker, they flew by, no sirens, but they were going fast!"

Cooker raced to the annex to knock on his assistant's door. After several tries went unanswered, he began to bang. Virgile finally responded and stood in the doorway in a white T-shirt and navy-blue boxer shorts with yellow polka dots. His eyes were half-closed, and his face bore the creases of his bedsheets. His mouth was frozen in a half yawn.

"You have five minutes to take a shower and meet me."

While he waited, Cooker went to drink a cup of tea without bothering to eat anything. He checked the inside pages of the *Le Bien Public*. Robert Bressel had written an evasive article mentioning only that the investigation was running its course, that some new clues had appeared, and that the police were following every lead. The journalist seemed to be trying to reassure readers, but his tone was almost clinical.

When Virgile tumbled into the dining room, Cooker did not even let him come to the table, where Aurélie had just laid out a generous breakfast. He led him directly to the road leading to the vineyard. They walked quickly without exchanging a word and soon arrived at the Château du Clos de Vougeot. Several vehicles were parked helter-skelter, and a crowd had formed in front of the heavy door. Police officers were talking quietly with a group of firefighters, while some other men in uniforms stood slightly apart, chatting with the farmhands. Cooker and Virgile approached cautiously.

A small owl was nailed to the enormous entry door. Its wings were spread apart to reveal a cavity of brown flesh swarming with maggots. The animal was in an advanced state of decay, and its mud-stained plumage had disappeared in certain places. On the left panel of the door, an enormous black inscription was written diagonally: "Jeremiah," and on the other side, below the bird, slightly skewed near the hinges, Cooker could make out "26."

"Mr. Cooker, how are you?"

Cooker swung around and recognized the head of the Confrérie des Chevaliers du Tastevin, who was walking toward him with his hand extended in a friendly gesture. Despite the worried expression that was darkening his face, the man could not neglect his good manners and natural cordiality.

"For heaven's sake, I'm very well, my friend, if it weren't for these unusual distractions."

"Since your arrival, it seems impossible to get a good night's sleep in Vougeot!"

"By that do you mean I am a bird of ill omen?" the winemaker allowed himself to joke as he introduced his assistant.

The Burgundian was delighted to see that the specialists from Bordeaux were so interested in the productions of the Côte-d'Or. He did not try to hide his satisfaction when they mentioned their recent wine tasting experiences and announced their desire to return soon.

"I am very sorry that you happened to arrive in the middle of such business," he said, chagrined. "I don't understand any of this."

"Oh, we've seen things like this before. Haven't we, Virgile?"

Virgile gave Cooker a knowing look.

"But who could this Jeremiah be?" continued the representative of the brotherhood. "Certainly not the author of all these senseless acts. He wouldn't sign his own crimes, would he? Could the culprit have wanted to expose someone named Jeremiah?"

"Who knows?" Cooker said, shrugging.

"I don't know of any Jeremiah in the vicinity. And I don't mean to brag, but I think I know Vougeot and its environs pretty well."

They reeled off pleasantries and useless theories, all in a tone of impeccable civility. But Cooker was preoccupied and in a hurry to leave. He was grateful for Virgile's intervention.

"I believe we are expected elsewhere, Mr. Cooker."

"Indeed, Virgile, duty calls."

They said good-bye with the utmost courtesy and headed back to the hotel.

"I think I know what it is, my boy."

"I suspected as much, boss."

"Really?"

"When I saw that frown, I knew right away."

"I didn't look too unpleasant, I hope?"

"It was close, but you were okay. But anyone who knows you well could tell."

"Thanks for letting me escape honorably."

"You're welcome. I was in a rush to go back myself. I still haven't had a bite to eat this morning."

"This Jeremiah doesn't exist," Cooker said without responding to his employee's remark. "He does not exist, or at least not the way they all think. It's that '26' that put me on the right track. At first I stupidly thought that it was about a guy who was twenty-six years old or maybe about someone who was born in 1926."

"That's not all that stupid. Maybe it's a simple clue. Why complicate things?"

"But who says it's complicated? Go and have your breakfast. I have two or three things to check in my room."

Cooker got back to the annex and rushed to his Bible. He went straight to the Book of the Prophets and stopped at Jeremiah, which was preceded by the words of Isaiah and announced "The Lamentations." The text contained fifty-two paragraphs, or two times twenty-six.

§ § §

As soon as he saw the drawn features and sad eyes of the abbey porter, Cooker understood that Brother Clément's health had deteriorated even further.

"Everything is going very quickly, Mr. Cooker. Since yesterday he has not been able to get out of bed, and I fear that he will not hear the bells of the next vespers."

"I do not want to bother him. Excuse me for coming so late, but I worked all afternoon at Charmots."

"I think it's one of Brother Clément's favorite Pommard wines. Do not be afraid. I know that he will be happy to see you."

They crossed the cloister and entered the large white stone stairway leading to the lodgings. At the end of a long corridor filled with shadows and silence, they came into a small cell, where a young monk was kneeling beside a bed. Brother Clément was lying on a white sheet, with a wool blanket pulled up to his waist. The porter signaled the novice to leave. Cooker walked slowly to keep the floorboards from creaking. He sat on a wooden stool at Brother Clément's bedside.

"It's good...of you to...I was waiting...for you."

His voice was extremely weak, as if emptied of all its substance, but a gleam still remained in his eyes. The winemaker leaned even closer.

"The tawny owl...the ruins..." stammered the monk, whose bloodless lips hardly moved.

"I thought about it," Cooker said almost in a whisper. "I reread the psalm many times before coming, but I still don't know what to deduce from it."

"All day long...my enemies...insult me..."

"Those who once praised me now use me as a curse," Cooker continued. He could have recited all of Psalm 102 in one breath, so much had he dwelled on it in his hotel room.

"It's...the prayer...of a...poor wretch..."

"Please don't strain yourself, Father. I have thought about all of it, and I, too, think that we are dealing with a desperate person. I also think he wanted to announce his revenge by pointing to Chapter Twenty-Six in the Book of Jeremiah. Because it can be nothing else, correct?"

Brother Clément closed his eyes twice to show that he agreed.

Cooker remained silent, wondering where the dying man was finding the energy to still take an interest in the land of the living.

With infinite tenderness, the abbey porter came in to touch the old man's forehead and feel his pulse. "He is asleep. He is still with us, but his body departs from time to time."

"The best would be if he did not awaken," murmured the winemaker.

"I don't believe so. He has always lived with his eyes wide open, lucid, and perceptive. He deserves to leave fully conscious."

"How long have you known him?"

"I was his student at the seminary before joining him in the cloister. He taught me everything. I have been entrusted with the duty of abbey porter for more than fifteen years now, and I owe this sign of trust from our abbot to the education that Brother Clément gave me. His courses were models of generosity and open mindedness. This is all that is required of an abbey porter."

"I am surprised that he talked to me about this psalm," Cooker whispered. "How did he know about the owl at the Château du Clos de Vougeot?"

"I've told you that he has always had great vision in this life. And it seems to me that he is still alive, no?"

"I am sure that he would have many things to tell me about that owl if he still had the strength."

"He would have said that it's an animal with an unfortunate reputation. It's been made an emblem of ugliness and a sign of bad fortune. In early days, you'd find them nailed like that in cemeteries or on farmhouse doors. Ignorant people believed they brought bad luck because they were night creatures. But living in the dark sharpens the ability to apprehend the unknown, to use one's mind to conquer the darkness. In a way, it's putting one's experience, knowledge, and thoughts in the service of wisdom. Men of the church are often described as crows. Some are, of course. But we others, the contemplatives who embrace seclusion and a certain solitude, we who get up at night to pray and earn the salvation of souls, we are, in a way, far-sighted owls!"

"How is it that I don't know your name?" Cooker suddenly asked.

"Because you've never asked," answered the monk. "My name is Brother Grégoire."

A door slammed in the distance. The noise, usually so mundane, had something incongruous about it, a violence that had no place in this environment. Brother Clément opened an eye and began to moan. Brother Grégoire pulled down the blanket and folded it over the end of the bed.

"He has nothing but the skin on his bones left, and the least bit of weight makes him suffer," he explained to Cooker, who was visibly worried.

"I don't see him breathing. Is he sleeping?"

"I think so. May the spirit of Saint Bernard accompany him in his sleep!"

"Are you talking about Saint Bernard, the monk at Cîteaux and founder of the Clairvaux Abbey?"

"I don't know any other by that name," Brother Grégoire replied, surprised. "Why would I pray to someone else? Saint Bernard slept very little. He spent enough time working each night to become the patron of all insomniacs, the patron saint of dream chasers."

Brother Clément cast his right eye in Cooker's direction. Cooker drew closer again to catch the snippets filtering from his dry lips.

"Read...me...the prophecies of...Jeremiah."

An old Bible was lying on the bedside table. Brother Grégoire handed it to Cooker, who put on his reading glasses. There were nearly one hundred pages in the Book of Jeremiah, and Cooker didn't know where to start.

"From the beginning," the porter instructed.

He read for more than an hour, without stopping, turning the pages at a regular rhythm like a penitent on a hard road. He read without worrying about whether his voice would soothe Brother Clément in this bare cell. He read the adventures of knowledge and violence, exile and corruption, the temple destruction, and foreign divinities. He read about promises of punishment and prophesies to the glory of man saved by the All Powerful. He read the lamentations until he became inebriated with words both nonsensical and sublime.

Yahweh says this: Look, I shall fill all
the inhabitants of this country, the kings
who occupy the throne of David, the
priests, the prophets and all the citizens
of Jerusalem, with drunkenness.

Then I shall smash them one against the
other, parents and children all together.

Yahweh declares. Mercilessly, relent-
lessly, pitilessly, I shall destroy them.

He was nearing the end of Chapter Thirteen when the bells of the Abbey of Cîteaux rang to announce vespers. Cooker shuddered and looked up to catch Brother Clément's serene gaze. He thought he saw a smile appear between the hollowed cheeks.

The dying man's lips quivered, and Cooker understood that he wanted to speak to him. He pressed his ear closer. The monk murmured a few words and then gave his soul up to God.

11

She was offering herself without shyness or modesty to Virgile's feverish fingers. He would never come back to see her, and for a moment, she must have dreamed that he would take her away from this place that she knew only too well, that he would take her to the ends of the earth. But Aurélie was a down-to-earth girl and settled for what Fate brought her. For a few days, it was this handsome boy with brown hair and brown eyes who was eagerly caressing her breasts. Virgile's fingers lingered a moment over her stomach, lightly brushing her navel, massaging the fullness of her hips. Then he slid his hands across her chest to titillate her nipples. She let him know she liked this little game of teasing by biting his earlobe. Virgile gave in to it in turn and let out a moan as soon as he felt Aurélie's hot breath between his thighs.

A few hours earlier, both of them had slipped out of the hotel to go dancing at a nightclub in Dijon whose Spanish-sounding name was not worth remembering. Cooker had been fast asleep, probably over a chapter of the Bible, so the night was theirs. They had escaped in Aurélie's tiny car and had drunk several glasses of cheap tequila, their heads already reeling from sufficiently adulterated German techno music.

Back in Vougeot, the girl told him she didn't want to end up spending the night in Virgile's bed, as she had been too embarrassed the night before coming out of his room when she ran into Cooker. She didn't want to see his amused look again. Despite Virgile's insistent pleas, she parked at the edge of town, out of sight, in the recesses of an overgrown dirt road.

Virgile was pressing tenderly on the nape of Aurélie's neck, matching her rhythmic movements. His mouth was on fire. If there was a God, he would have to reside in the body of a woman, he thought. After performing the delicate ritual of the condom, which almost turned into a comedy, the girl seated herself on Virgile's lap, facing and embracing him. She was holding onto the seat while she straddled him, letting out frightened squeals. They hadn't found any other solution for making love in the cramped Fiat 500, whose original pistachio color and rust-dotted chrome authenticated its rare 1962 vintage.

Aurélie had snuggled against his shoulder and was nibbling on his neck. Now they were satisfied, entwined in their shared sweatiness, unable to separate. For a long while Virgile kept his eyes closed. When he finally opened them, he thought he saw a dark impression standing against a pale moon. He blinked to probe the darkness. The shadow was in profile, one arm raised on the side of a barn. He pushed Aurélie aside brusquely and threw his clothes on helter-skelter. The girl watched dumbfounded and teary-eyed as he opened the car door and started dashing toward the town. He ran full speed on the soggy path and almost slid as he rounded a patch of vines. In front of him, the silhouette was weaving between a cluster of shrubs and bolting toward the Vouge River flowing below. Virgile was closing in. The fugitive hesitated to head down the streets of Vougeot, deciding instead to return to the twists and turns of the vineyard.

"Keep going, you idiot!" Virgile yelled, energized by the memory of muddy practices on the rugby field in Montravel.

It took him just a few seconds to catch up to the man, who had begun limping. Virgile tackled him, crashing down with all his weight. They rolled in a water-filled rut. The fight was quickly over. His two knees pressed against his adversary's torso, Virgile prepared to deliver a punch, but his arm froze.

The man was a woman.

§ § §

"And where were you again, Virgile?" Benjamin Cooker said, glancing at the side mirror as he pulled out skillfully, and passed a Dutch camper.

"In her car, sir."

"The green one that looks like a Burgundy escargot?"

"That's funny, I thought the same thing."

"It's an old model, rather sought-after, but not very practical for a strapping young man like yourself."

Virgile ignored the remark and continued telling his story: the chase in the middle of the vines, a tackle worthy of rugby star Serge Blanco, the scuffle in the mud, and his shock when he discovered the frightened face of Murielle Grangeon.

"The police told me her name while I was giving my deposition, but I still didn't understand any of it. They didn't see fit to fill me in."

"I got Robert Bressel on the phone while you were being questioned," Cooker confided. "Trust a reporter to find what the police don't know yet. He knew this Murielle Grangeon very well."

"Is she related to the old Adèle?"

"She's her niece, a poor girl who's been struggling for years. She started off okay, studying classical languages and medieval history. She loved that stuff. She went to school with

Bressel's nephew Pierre-Jean. She was majoring in Latin and Greek and getting her master's in twelfth-century monastic studies in the dukedom of Burgundy. But then she got knocked up and married some guy from Gilly who used to beat her. It seems like he made a living doing odd jobs and selling stolen cars. He's in prison now, sentenced to eight years. So she found herself alone with two kids. She cleaned offices at night for a commercial cleaning company in Dijon."

"And the kids?" Virgile interrupted. "Did she leave them home alone?"

"No, she lived with her mother, at the other end of Vougeot."

"So her mother is Adèle Grangeon's sister?"

"No, her sister-in-law. Murielle's father was Adèle's brother. The guy died very young of a heart attack. Do you follow me?"

"Up to this point, it's simple. So, in short, the kids' grandmother was a widow and took care of them while Murielle slaved away at a crappy job."

"I imagine she must have felt frustrated having left behind her classical studies for a life of menial labor," Virgile said.

"Not only did she have to work hard, but then her mother got sick. Some kind of cancer, which killed her in just a few months. She had to leave her job to take care of the kids. With no money, no job, and mouths to feed, the first thought Murielle had was to go to her aunt Adèle. But the old lady wouldn't even put them up. Nothing, no helping hand. Door shut, get lost."

"What a bitch! Excuse me, but there's no other word."

"I agree completely."

"So she found herself on the street?" Virgile asked, worried.

"At first, not really. Some friends from school took her in here and there, but you know how that goes. After a certain amount of time, there aren't too many friends who can put up with two kids and a mother in a small apartment. She ended up in a home for single mothers and women in distress. You know the type of place. She was offered unappealing and underpaid internships. Nothing to meet her needs, and the Department of Health and Social Services put her kids in foster homes. That's when she had her first bout of major depression."

"That could put anyone over the edge," Virgile said sympathetically.

Cooker glanced at the wobbling arrow at the bottom of the gas gauge. He would have to fill the tank of his SL280 soon if he didn't want to force Virgile to spend another night under the stars. He took his foot off the gas pedal and continued driving at a more reasonable speed.

"But Mr. Cooker, when you say that she had her first bout of depression, you mean that she had many more?"

"Yes, she was diagnosed as manic-depressive. She was treated with her fair share of antidepressants, antianxiety pills, tranquilizers, and sleeping pills. And she spent long periods in psychiatric hospitals. According to Bressel, she changed enormously during that period. She was getting thinner and exhibiting strange behavior. She seemed to be changing more and more every day."

"And the kids?"

"She saw them once or twice a month. And even then, only if her condition allowed. She did have one opportunity, though, thanks to Pierre-Jean Bressel. When he heard that a job as a guide had opened up at the Château du Clos de Vougeot, he had his uncle Robert pull some strings to get her foot in the door. Of course, she landed it easily. She knew the history by heart, and what's more, she was from the area."

"All's well that ends well, then."

"Not really. She thought things would get better. But the Department of Health and Social Services wouldn't let her have her kids back. They said her situation wasn't yet stable, that she didn't have suitable housing or a long-term contract. That didn't help her mental health, and she had several more crises. She started showing up for work late and taking sick days. Eventually, she hardly showed up at all. The château could not renew her contract."

"She must have been angry at the world."

"Let's say, rather, that her depression turned to anger. With her situation becoming more and more precarious and her unemployment checks running out, the manic-depression became more acute. She had short periods of overexcitement alternating with moments of extreme withdrawal. Murielle soon lost her sense of reality. A specialist could explain it better than I can."

"Don't worry, boss. Crazy is crazy."

"You do have a skill for distilling things," Cooker said, smiling, "even if that's a bit harsh."

They stopped at a gas station and filled the tank. While his boss cleaned the windshield, Virgile got out to stretch his legs, flirt with the cashier, and buy a copy of the sports newspaper *L'Equipe*. As they were leaving, Cooker turned on his cassette player and invited *La Traviata* to accompany them on the trip.

"That's all we need now!" exclaimed Virgile. "You know I don't care for opera, and honestly, this Maria Callas woman scares me a little. I don't know why, but she sends shivers down my spine."

"I would be disappointed if you said she didn't, my boy. Callas touches the deepest part of what we are."

"Was your diva another tormented soul?"

"I don't think so. Let's just say she had a flair for the dramatic."

"Is the whole story that you told me just the reporter's version?"

"Yes. On the other hand, it was the investigators who uncovered the rest. At least, what they were able to piece together, because even with the help of the experts, it's hard to interrogate someone like that. When she wrote her first messages in Vougeot and Gilly, she was in the middle of a manic phase, and she surely did that in a delirium of vengeance inspired by a desire to frighten people. I think she must have been angry with the whole world, but her world had been reduced to that little corner of vineyard where she endured all the suffering and humiliation."

"But why phrases from the Bible?"

"In my opinion, she must have had a mystical vision of the world. All that time spent on ancient texts, translating from Latin, steeped morning, noon, and night in obscure religious writing, stories of sorcerers, ghosts, demons."

"That couldn't have been good for her! Do you think that's why she did what she did?"

"I do. When she wanted to terrorize her aunt, all she did was reproduce some very old scenes from Burgundy folklore. She knew them inside out. On each occasion she used the situation to her own advantage. Old Mancenot, for example. She just happened to come across him. She was getting ready to write some ominous messages when she spotted his moped on the side of the road. Honoré was so drunk, he had had a fatal accident. The findings from the investigation and

137

autopsy confirm it. Murielle, as delirious as she was, knew how to turn the event into something malevolent. Same thing with the owl: she found it while she was roaming the town at night. The bird had already been dead for quite a while, which explains the condition it was in, but she knew how to turn it into an object of terror. I don't even want to imagine what was going through her mind in moments like that."

"What is she up against, now?" Virgile asked, somewhat worried.

"Compared to what she has been through, she's not in danger anymore. She'll be able to get better treatment. After all, she didn't kill anyone. She'll surely be charged with disturbing the peace and defacing private property. But in my opinion, her mental state will be taken into consideration."

"And yet, two teens were slain because of her, in a way. That's the worst thing, it seems to me."

"Indeed, that's the most tragic part of the whole story. Their burial is next Monday in Gilly, and there may be a big turnout. Robert Bressel will have his front-page article."

Cooker flashed his headlights to keep a Spanish truck from cutting him off while passing. The road sign announced that Bordeaux was four hundred and fifty miles away, and the night promised to be a long one.

"In my opinion, the librarian had guessed the whole thing," Cooker continued, putting on the windshield wipers. "He knew Murielle Grangeon well enough and was aware that there were few individuals capable of quoting the Psalms of David and the Book of the Prophets by heart and knowing the old local traditions as well as she did. I do not deny that I suspected him of being involved in some way. After all, he also had sufficient motives for wanting revenge."

"I personally think that it was honorable of him to say nothing," Virgile murmured.

"Maybe Brother Clément had also guessed a lot of things. Murielle had often consulted him during her research. When I think back on everything that he told me, there were actually lots of clues to put me on the right track. Pierre-Jean Bressel emphasized the presence of children in all of the haunted-house stories. Brother Clément always brought me back to the themes of the vine, sorrow, and injustice, as if he were trying to steer me in the right direction. And then there was the owl reference that could have been read as a pelican, which relates to the sacrifice of mothers. Perhaps I should have known that we weren't necessarily dealing with a man."

"What did the monk say to you when he was dying?"

"*Honora Dominum et vino torcularia redundabunt.*"

"And what does that mean?"

"Honor the Lord, and vats will overflow with wine."

"Magnificent! Imagine. His last word was 'wine.' I would love to die that way," Virgile said with a yawn.

"Not really, his last word was '*redundabunt*' because you always place the verb at the end of a sentence in Latin. As for the rest, the question is not so much knowing what you say at the moment of death but how you say it."

La Traviata took off on a thrilling flight that the violins could not bring back to earth.

"You see, Virgile, we wandered in the age of the Pharisees, in the footsteps of the apostles and the mystic Jews. We experienced the tonsure of Cîteaux and the dungeons of the Middle Ages. We even came close to believing in the devil and ghosts, and finally, it was nothing but a modern story: divorced unemployed mother no longer entitled to benefits, children taken away, court orders. Hopelessly modern!"

Cooker turned to look at his assistant. Virgile had fallen asleep. He was snoring peacefully, his mouth half open like an angel. Cooker swerved a bit as he reached for his coat to cover his passenger. Then he lowered the volume of *La Traviata* until she didn't have a breath of life left in her.

"Sweet dreams, my boy. Come the night, all is forgotten."

Thank you for reading Nightmare in Burgundy.

We invite you to share your thoughts and reactions on Goodreads and your favorite social media and retail platforms.

We appreciate your support.

THE WINEMAKER DETECTIVE SERIES

A total Epicurean immersion in French countryside and gourmet attitude with two expert winemakers turned amateur sleuths gumshoeing around wine country. The following titles are currently available in English.

Treachery in Bordeaux

The start of this wine plus crime mystery series, this journey to Bordeaux takes readers behind the scenes of a grand cru wine estate that has fallen victim to either negligence or sabotage. World-renowned winemaker turned gentleman detective Benjamin Cooker sets out to find out what happened and why. Who would want to target this esteemed vintner?

www.treacheryinbordeaux.com

Grand Cru Heist

In another Epicurean journey in France, renowned wine critic Benjamin Cooker's world gets turned upside down one night in Paris. He retreats to the region around Tours to recover. There a flamboyant British dandy, a spectacular blue-eyed blond, a zealous concierge, and touchy local police disturb his well-deserved rest. From the Loire Valley to Bordeaux, in between a glass of Vouvray and a bottle of Saint-Émilion, the Winemaker Detective and his assistant Virgile turn PI to solve two murders and very particular heist. Who stole those bottles of grand cru classé?

www.grandcruheist.com

Deadly Tasting

A serial killer stalks Bordeaux, signing his crimes with a strange ritual. To understand the wine-related symbolism, the local police call on the famous wine critic Benjamin Cooker. The investigation leads them to the dark hours of France's history, as the mystery thickens among the once-peaceful vineyards of Pomerol.

www.deadlytasting.com

ABOUT THE AUTHORS

Noël Balen (left) and Jean-Pierre Alaux (right).
(©David Nakache)

Jean-Pierre Alaux and **Noël Balen** came up with the Winemaker Detective over a glass of wine, of course. Jean-Pierre Alaux is a magazine, radio, and television journalist when he is not writing novels in southwestern France. He is a genuine wine and food lover, and won the Antonin Carême prize for his cookbook *La Truffe sur le Soufflé*, which he wrote with the chef Alexis Pélissou. He is the grandson of a winemaker and exhibits a real passion for wine and winemaking. For him, there is no greater common denominator than wine. Coauthor of the series Noël Balen lives in Paris, where he shares his time between writing, making records, and lecturing on music. He plays bass, is a music critic, and has authored a number of books about musicians, in addition to his novel and short-story writing.

ABOUT THE TRANSLATOR

Sally Pane studied French at State University of New York Oswego and the Sorbonne before receiving her master's degree in French literature from the University of Colorado where she wrote *Camus and the Americas: A Thematic Analysis of Three Works Based on His Journaux de Voyage*. Her career includes more than twenty years of translating and teaching French and Italian at Berlitz and at Colorado University Boulder. She has worked in scientific, legal and literary translation; her literary translations include *Operatic Arias; Singers Edition,* and *Reality and the Untheorizable* by Clément Rosset. She also served as the interpreter for the government cabinet of Rwanda and translated for Dian Fossey's Digit Fund. In addition to her passion for French, she has studied Italian at Colorado University, in Rome and in Siena. She lives in Boulder, Colorado, with her husband.

Discover more books from

Le French Book

www.lefrenchbook.com

The 7th Woman by Frédérique Molay

An edge-of-your-seat mystery set in Paris, where beautiful sounding names surround ugly crimes that have Chief of Police Nico Sirsky and his team on tenterhooks.

www.the7thwoman.com

The Paris Lawyer by Sylvie Granotier

A psychological thriller set between the sophisticated corridors of Paris and a small backwater in central France, where rolling hills and quiet country life hide dark secrets.

www.theparislawyer.com

The Greenland Breach by Bernard Besson

The Arctic ice caps are breaking up. Europe and the East Coast of the United States brace for a tidal wave. A team of freelance spies face a merciless war for control of discoveries that will change the future of humanity.

www.thegreenlandbreach.com

The Bleiberg Project by David Khara

Are Hitler's atrocities really over? Find out in this adrenaline-pumping ride to save the world from a conspiracy straight out of the darkest hours of history.

www.thebleibergproject.com

CPSIA information can be obtained
at www.ICGtesting.com
Printed in the USA
LVOW10s0359061216
515960LV00011B/58/P